"To what do I owe this unexpected visit?" Max asked.

"I'm here to ask you out to dinner."

He couldn't have been more shocked if Ashley had walked into his office and started a striptease. "Why?"

"Do I need a reason?" she asked, hedging.

Throwing caution to the wind, he stood and walked around his desk. He was close enough to pull her into his arms. She met his gaze and took several steps back.

"Yeah." He crossed his arms. "Why don't you sit down and tell me what information you're trying to worm out of me?"

She nodded.

As she settled herself, the whisper of her nylons as she crossed one shapely leg over the other sent sparks skipping through him. Her skirt hiked up several inches on her thigh.

She didn't have to buy him dinner to find out his secrets.

All she had to do was sit there looking like sin-in-waiting.

Dear Reader,

Here is an acronym that explains why you should not miss the opportunity to enjoy four new love stories from Silhouette Romance so close to Valentine's Day:

L is for the **l**ast title in Silhouette Romance's delightful MARRYING THE BOSS'S DAUGHTER six-book continuity. So far, Emily Winters has thwarted her father's attempts to marry her off. But has Daddy's little girl finally met her matrimonial match? Find out in *One Bachelor To Go* (#1706) by Nicole Burnham.

O is for the **o**rnery cowboy who's in for a life change when he is forced to share his home...and his heart with a gun-toting single mom and her kids, in Patricia Thayer's *Wyatt's Ready-Made Family* (#1707). It's the latest title in Thayer's continuing THE TEXAS BROTHERHOOD miniseries.

V is for the great **v**ibes you'll get from Teresa Southwick's *Flirting With the Boss* (#1708). This is the second title of Southwick's IF WISHES WERE... terrific new miniseries in which three friends' wishes magically come true.

E is for the **e**motion you'll feel as you read *Saved by the Baby* (#1709) by Linda Goodnight. In this heartwarming story, a desperate young mother's quest to save her daughter's life leads her back to the child's father, her first and only love.

Read all four of these fabulous stories. I guarantee they'll get you in the mood for *l-o-v-e!*

Mavis C. Allen
Associate Senior Editor

Flirting With the Boss

TERESA SOUTHWICK

Published by Silhouette Books
America's Publisher of Contemporary Romance

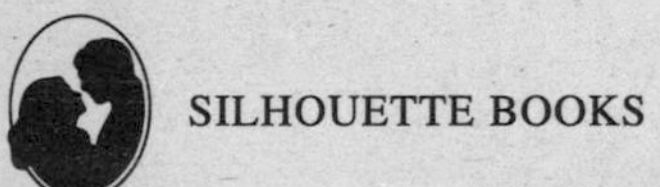

ISBN 0-373-19708-X

FLIRTING WITH THE BOSS

This edition published by arrangement with Harlequin Books S.A.

Visit Silhouette at www.eHarlequin.com

Printed in U.S.A.

Books by Teresa Southwick

Silhouette Romance

Wedding Rings and Baby Things #1209
The Bachelor's Baby #1233
**A Vow, a Ring, a Baby Swing* #1349
The Way to a Cowboy's Heart #1383
**And Then He Kissed Me* #1405
**With a Little T.L.C.* #1421
The Acquired Bride #1474
**Secret Ingredient: Love* #1495
**The Last Marchetti Bachelor* #1513
***Crazy for Lovin' You* #1529
***This Kiss* #1541
***If You Don't Know by Now* #1560
***What If We Fall in Love?* #1572
Sky Full of Promise #1624
†*To Catch a Sheik* #1674
†*To Kiss a Sheik* #1686
†*To Wed a Sheik* #1696
††*Baby, Oh Baby!* #1704
††*Flirting With the Boss* #1708

*The Marchetti Family
**Destiny, Texas
†Desert Brides
††If Wishes Were…

Silhouette Books

The Fortunes of Texas
Shotgun Vows

Silhouette Special Edition

The Summer House #1510
"Courting Cassandra"
Midnight, Moonlight & Miracles #1517

TERESA SOUTHWICK

lives in Southern California with her hero husband who is more than happy to share with her the male point of view. An avid fan of romance novels, she is delighted to be living out her dream of writing for Silhouette Books.

The Fortune-teller said…

Money and power are not
what they seem. Love is the sweetness
that brings you your dream.

If the three born on February twenty-ninth
rub the magic from the lamp and
make a wish—on that day that comes
only once every four years—each shall
receive her most coveted desire.

But there is peril.

Each of the three must see beyond the evident.
Look into the soul of the one
her heart has chosen.
Only then will she find the truth
that is hers alone.

Chapter One

Sweet Spring, Texas—June 4, 2004

All that glitters…

Is not gold, Ashley Gallagher thought. She stared at the gold-wrapped chocolate coins on her desk—one of Caine Chocolate Company's specialty items. Bentley Caine, owner, president and her mentor, had recently promoted her to manager of the specialty and seasonal department.

Touching the red ribbon tied around the cellophane package, she thought about the man who was also her friend. He was in the hospital recuperating from a heart attack. After collapsing at work, he'd insisted she contact his estranged grandson.

Max Caine wasn't the last person she'd wanted to talk to, but he was among the bottom three. Only her respect and affection for his grandfather had compelled her to make the call.

She'd given him the facts. Max had made no attempt to draw out the conversation so she'd said goodbye. That had been two days ago. She wasn't sure what she'd expected from him, but her expectations hadn't included nothing. Surely by now Max should have—

''Knock, knock.''

Ashley looked up at the sound of the masculine voice. Her stomach knotted when she recognized the good-looking specimen of manhood in the doorway. Just the man she'd been thinking about. A stress-inducer if she'd ever seen one. Unfortunately she'd seen her share. This one had just been the first.

''Hello, Max.'' Her voice was breathless. Considering she'd barely gotten the two words past the constriction in her throat, breathless delivery was a win.

''Ashley.'' Max Caine moved into the room. ''How are you?''

How brazen was he? Acting as if it had been ten days instead of ten years since she'd last seen him. Swallowing hard, she met his blue-eyed gaze. If only she could say she'd forgotten how blue his eyes were, but she couldn't. Not if she was truthful.

And darn her heart for thumping so hard. The fact that he was even better looking than the last time she'd seen him was no excuse for this reaction to him. She could only chalk it up to the fact that she was a serial non-dater.

But gosh darn it, Max Caine had actually come back. She hadn't thought he would. Neither had Mr. Caine. While they'd waited for the paramedics, he'd said he wanted to see his grandson. But he didn't think Max would come if he did the asking. He'd insisted she make the call to bring Max home. Mission accomplished.

"How am I? How do you think after your grandfather's heart attack? How is he today?"

"I haven't seen him yet." Max rested his palms on her desk and leaned forward, frowning as he studied her. "I'm here looking for my grandfather, Ashley."

"Have you *looked* for him at Sweet Spring General Hospital?" she asked.

"He's not there." Exasperation coated his words.

"That's impossible. He was just moved to a regular room from the cardiac care unit yesterday. The doctor said he wanted to keep Mr. Caine in the hospital at least a few more days."

"Apparently he left."

She blinked. "Why would he do that?"

"Your guess is as good as mine." Max lifted one broad shoulder. "I'm just passing on the information I was given."

Ashley stared at him, then picked up her phone. "Bernice, get Mr. Caine's cardiologist on the phone."

"Right away," came the female voice on the other end of the line.

Ashley set the receiver back in the cradle and looked up. "I don't understand. Who did you speak to at the hospital?"

"Does it matter?"

"Maybe. Patients get moved. It's possible you were given the wrong room number."

"Are you suggesting I should have searched every room?"

"I'm just saying, maybe you only talked to someone at the information desk who hadn't been updated yet about a move."

"A move that happened yesterday? News in the hospital travels by pony express?"

He had a point, but wild horses wouldn't compel her to tell him that. "I can't believe he would do this." The phone buzzed, and she picked it up. When she was told the doctor was on line two, she pressed the button and said, "Doctor Davis? Ashley Gallagher here."

"How can I help you, Miss Gallagher?"

"It's about Mr. Caine." She looked up at the other Mr. Caine staring intently at her and tried to ignore the jittery feeling his gaze generated inside her.

"Yes?"

"I've just been told he's no longer in the hospital."

"That's right. He walked out."

"But how could you let him do that?"

"I can't force a patient to stay. I can only make sure he understands the seriousness of his condition. Are you calling from work?"

"Yes."

"So he's not there?"

Her eyes widened. "I haven't seen him, but that doesn't mean—"

"If he is, I advise you to make him go home."

"And what makes you think I would have more luck with him than you did?"

The chuckle on the other end of the line was tinged with dark humor. "Good point. I wish you luck anyway. He's a stubborn old man. But I like him."

"Me, too," she said.

"If there's anything I can do, let me know."

"Can I call on you if I need some muscle?" She looked at the muscular man whose gaze had been superglued to her this whole time. But Max had disappeared from Bentley Caine's life ten years ago. There was no reason to believe she could count on him for help now.

The doctor laughed, this time in genuine amusement. "I'll do whatever I can, Miss Gallagher."

"Thank you," she said, then hung up the phone. Looking up at Max she said, "You're right. He's AWOL. Have you checked the house?" she asked.

"Right after the hospital. No sign of him," he said, sliding his big hands into the pockets of his suit slacks.

Expensive slacks unless she missed her guess. The supremely masculine movement upset the sleek, perfect line of the costly matching jacket. His beige dress shirt and coordinating geometric-patterned tie were immaculate, unlike the memories he'd left behind.

"Have you checked his office?" She stood up.

Her simmering exasperation at the senior Mr. Caine escalated. If he ignored his cardiologist's advice to rest in the hospital after a heart attack, what would prevent that stubborn old man from sneaking back to work against his doctor's orders? Without waiting for an answer, she rounded her desk and headed out the door.

Max Caine fell into step beside her as she walked down the hall. He was tall, much taller than his grandfather, about six feet to her five feet three inches, unless she missed her guess. He was more filled out through the chest than she remembered. And his hair was different. Unlike the too-long shaggy style she'd last seen, now his sandy blond hair was short and neatly combed. But his strong, square jaw and the nose that was neither too big nor too small for his face were the same. He was still very attractive, but now instead of radiating bad boy boldness, he was too-smooth, too-*GQ,* too-businessman chic.

She admitted to herself that she was judging him without mercy. That couldn't be helped. Men who left without saying goodbye didn't deserve mercy. Granted, she'd been a fourteen-year-old with a raging crush, but his indifference had cut deep. She'd gotten over it. What she couldn't forgive was not a single word to his grandfather in a decade. That indifference had devastated the older man who was her friend as well as her boss. Anyone who hurt him had to answer to her.

She stopped at the end of the hall in front of the receptionist. "Bernice, have you seen Mr. Caine today?"

The thirty-something brunette met her gaze, then slid an appreciative, appraising look to the man beside Ashley. "Isn't he still in the hospital?"

Ashley glanced up at Max. "Apparently not," she said grimly.

"He's supposed to be."

"I know," Ashley admitted.

"Who's he?" Bernice asked, nodding toward Max.

"Max Caine," he said, extending his large hand.

The secretary's eyes widened as she put her palm in his. "The rebel?"

"Is that what they call me?" he asked Ashley.

"Among other things," she admitted.

"What other things?"

She felt the heat crawl up her neck. The question made her uncomfortable in spite of the fact she didn't feel the slightest inclination to spare this man's feelings or impress him. Unfortunately, she couldn't seem to stop the blush. She blew out a breath. "To everyone over thirty-five in this town you're the ingrate."

He glanced at Bernice who was barely concealing the fact that she thought he was hot. "And to everyone under thirty-five I'm the rebel?"

"You gotta love small towns." Ashley decided the opinion poll regarding Max Caine was skewed because she'd pitched her tent in the over thirty-five camp. "Bernice, it's come to my attention that Mr. *Bentley* Caine is unaccounted for. I'll just take a peek in his office in case he slipped past you."

"Be my guest," she said.

Ashley, with Max beside her, walked to the closed door and opened it. The oak-panelled, hunter green carpeted room was empty.

"Darn." She glanced up at Max who had easily looked over her head and came to the same conclusion she had. His grandfather wasn't there. "Now what?" she said to no one in particular.

A muscle in Max's jaw contracted. "Now we go look for him."

"What's this 'we' stuff?" she asked.

"Do you know his routine? His hangouts? His habits?"

"Yes, some, but—"

"Then I need you," he said, encircling her upper arm in his firm grip. "*We* is you and me."

"Where are you taking me?"

"To join the search party." Max frowned as he studied her, but it was impossible to tell what he was thinking.

"That's presumptuous. You don't know me from a rock—"

"Sure I do. You're the one who called and got me into this. Besides, I recognized you right away."

She knew better than to be pleased by that piece of information. But pleased she was. She reminded herself it didn't mean anything. "I didn't mean my looks. Besides, I haven't changed all that much."

"Sure you have. You've grown up since that summer we were friends."

She'd thought they were friends, but she'd found out differently. Her stomach clenched, and she pushed the feelings away. "The past isn't important."

"You won't get any argument from me about that. And now I'm asking for your help to find him."

"How come you're so concerned all of a sudden?" she demanded.

"How do you know it's sudden?"

She shrugged. "Logical conclusion based on your actions."

"My actions? Like coming back?"

"Your actions—as in you left and haven't *been* back in ten years. Why show up now? And I don't buy it's because you care that he's sick."

Lines creased his forehead, and he seemed lost in thought. "That's a very good question."

"And I'm waiting for a very good answer."

"I don't really have one. But when I do, you'll be the first to know."

"Actually your grandfather deserves the answer, not me. But if we don't find him—"

"We will."

Ashley thought there was an edge to Max's voice.

In anyone else, she might think it was caused by worry. But this was the guy who had turned his back a decade ago.

"I need to get my purse," she said, as they stopped outside her office. She was choosing to go with Max Caine because it was almost quitting time and she wouldn't get any work done now anyway. Not until her boss was located. "And my organizer."

"Does he use a cell phone?"

He? What did Max call Bentley Caine? Grandpa? Grampy? She looked at the tension in his square jaw and decided that would be a negative on Grampy. Grandfather?

She thought back to their conversations in the employee lunch room. At fourteen, she'd vented feelings of frustration about being grounded and having to go to work with her mother when she wasn't in summer school. Max had called her Mona the Moaner. He'd done his share of moaning. His grandfather was the source of major frustration. He'd talked about—Bentley.

He'd called the older man by his given name, and she'd thought it very cool—sophisticated. She'd had stars in her eyes because the larger-than-life rebel and hunk, Max Caine, had actually spent time with her. Then his actions had said loud and clear that she wasn't worth the spit it would take to let her know he was leaving town.

Now he had to ask her if his grandfather had a cell phone. Max should have come back. Then he would know the answer to that question.

"Ashley? It's not that difficult a question."

"No, your grandfather doesn't have a cell phone," she finally answered.

Max's mouth thinned to a grim line. "I had a feeling."

"A feeling?" The man was his family. He shouldn't have to rely on feelings. He should have been around all these years to know the facts. Then he wouldn't need her to steer him to his grandfather's hangouts. And just maybe if Max hadn't left, his grandfather wouldn't have worked himself into a heart attack. "You haven't seen him for ten years. How can you have feelings?"

"A figure of speech. It's more like informed intuition. Ten years ago he was stubborn, opinionated and dictatorial. And those were his good qualities." Max politely opened and held for her one of the double glass doors in the lobby. "I have no reason to believe he's changed."

"Is that so?" She walked past him and wasn't certain if the heat she felt was from him or the June air that made Sweet Spring, Texas, feel as hot as the face of the sun.

Ashley met his gaze. "Hmm. Stubborn, opinionated and dictatorial. Has anyone ever told you the fruit doesn't fall far from the tree?"

Chapter Two

Scrappy. Max looked down at Ashley Gallagher and that was the first word that came to mind. She was scrappy, all right, and if not for her phone call, he wouldn't be here.

Studying her he said, "Did you just insult me?"

"If you have to ask, I was too subtle."

He took her elbow and steered her toward his car parked in Caine Chocolate Company's lot. Heat was radiating in waves, and he couldn't decide if it was only from the blacktop or if some of it was coming from his companion.

"I'll drive," he said, stopping beside the silver BMW he'd rented at the airport. He opened the passenger door and Ashley slid inside. "You tell me where to go."

She looked up at him and rolled her eyes. "At least make it interesting. Don't just hand me gift-wrapped zingers."

He wanted to ask why she felt the need to zing him. But that was a conversation he didn't want to have while the Texas sun was frying his brain. "I'll rephrase. You keep your eyes open for the old man."

When she opened her mouth, he shut the door, then walked around the back of the car and let himself in on the driver's side. After cranking up the A/C full blast, he pulled out of the lot and headed for downtown Sweet Spring. Whatever she'd been about to say remained a mystery. Ashley didn't utter a word, but he could almost feel her thought waves vibrating.

He put on his left blinker, then stopped at the red light. Sliding a glance toward the passenger seat, he noticed she was rigid enough to snap. A few freckles dotted her turned-up nose, her pale skin looked perfect, making the red curls brushing her cheek blaze even brighter. Her profile was delicate and feminine, at odds with the unisex navy blue business suit she wore. The last time he'd seen her, she'd been a kid in the company cafeteria. Now she worked for his grandfather. He wondered if *she'd* ever disappointed Bentley Caine.

"Why did you call me?" he asked.

"Because your grandfather was ill, and he asked me to."

"He was well enough to walk out of the hospital. One has to assume he could have managed a phone. So why did you do the honors?"

She glanced over at him, then her gaze slid away. "Because he wanted to see you, and he said if *he* called, you wouldn't come."

He was right, Max thought. He was only here now out of a sense of duty. The same reason his grandfather had taken him in after his parents died. His conversation with Ashley had been short. She'd informed him that his grandfather's heart attack had put the old man in the cardiac care unit at Sweet Spring General Hospital. Then she'd given him the facility's phone number and told him Bentley Caine would like to see him.

Max's initial reaction had been to hang up. But some quality in Ashley's voice—a hint of gravel mixed with whiskey and liberally laced with hostility—had stopped him. After leaving town, he hadn't thought much about her. But when she identified herself on the other end of the line, memories had flooded back. He remembered a sweet, smiling kid. The picture in his head didn't mesh with the cool, cranky woman beside him.

She turned suddenly to look at a pedestrian on her side of the car, then faced front again. "I think we should go to the sheriff and file a missing person's report."

"It's my understanding that we have to wait at least twenty-four hours before he's officially considered missing." He glanced over at her. "Where does he like to go?"

"For fun?"

"My grandfather doesn't do fun. At least he didn't used to. I meant is there a favorite restaurant we can check? A hangout?"

The corners of her full mouth curved up. "I can't picture Mr. Caine hanging out. But his top three favorite places are Tiny's BBQ, Dairy Queen and The Fast Lane—it's a coffee shop in the bowling alley."

They were just passing the bowling alley, and he

made a hard right turn into the driveway. ''Let's take a look.''

When the BMW was parked, she got out and gave the lot the once-over. ''I don't see his car.''

''Maybe someone inside has seen him.''

As they walked side by side to the double glass doors, she glanced at him curiously. He could almost hear the questions echoing in her head. It was just a matter of time until she started asking them.

''Why are you doing this?'' she asked.

And there was the first one. ''Define this.''

''Don't play dumb, Max. We both know you're not. And before you ask, that wasn't a compliment. Just a statement of fact. Why are you bothering to look for your grandfather?''

''I came here to see him because I owe him that much. As soon as we find him, I can leave. It's that simple.''

Before she could make something out of that, they stopped at the bowling alley registration desk.

Ashley put her hands on the counter. ''Hi, Sam.''

''Ashley.'' The fit and forty-something dark-haired man standing there, studied him, openly curious.

''Sam Fisher this is Max Caine,'' she said.

''Sam,'' he said, shaking hands. ''I'm looking for my grandfather, Bentley Caine. Ashley tells me he likes to come in here.''

Sam's face flickered with recognition, but unlike Bernice, he managed to hold back the ingrate remarks. ''I know who he is. My wife works over at the chocolate factory.''

''I see. Have you seen him in the last twenty-four hours?''

Sam looked surprised. ''Isn't he in the hospital? I heard he had a heart attack.''

Ashley tucked a strand of copper-colored hair behind her ear. ''Mr. Caine walked out of the hospital sometime last night and no one has seen him. We're checking out the places he might have gone.''

''Sorry. He hasn't been here since I came in this morning. But I'll ask around.'' The other man shrugged. ''If he comes in, I'll let you know.''

''Okay,'' she said.

They started to back away when Sam added, ''He's a good guy. Always says we have the best fried chicken he's ever tasted.''

Max looked at him. ''And afterward, he can bowl a couple of games to counteract the blast of cholesterol.''

''Thanks, Sam.'' Ashley took Max's arm and aimed him toward the door. ''Way to get the sympathy vote, Ace. You could have gone all day without telling Sam Fisher his chicken is a heart attack waiting to happen.''

''Even though I said it with a great deal of charm?'' he asked.

''Here's a suggestion. When we check out the Dairy Queen and Tiny's BBQ, either we just cruise the parking lot or I go in alone. If you tell them they're a hotbed of heart disease, you're not likely to enlist their help in this endeavor.''

''Whatever you say.''

When they were back in the car driving through downtown Sweet Spring Ashley sighed like a balloon losing air.

''Spit it out before you implode,'' he said.

She didn't even pretend to misunderstand. "You know, diet isn't the only contributing factor in a heart attack."

"Lack of exercise, maybe?"

"I was thinking more along the lines of the strain of running Caine Chocolate all by himself."

"He's not alone. He's got you."

"True. I'm part of the administrative staff in place to manage the company. But I think you know that's not what I meant."

"How long have you worked there?" he asked.

"Since I was sixteen. It was my first job."

He glanced over at her. "So you worked your way through the ranks."

"Yes. And I try to take some of the stress off him. But I'm not family."

"I feel a zinger coming on."

"Another source of tension and pressure could be the desertion of a family member and his subsequent refusal to return home."

That was damned irritating. Her version of events was so slanted he couldn't help wondering if she was merely being a devoted employee paid to recite the company line. Or if she believed what she was saying. Because there was another side to the story. His side.

"How much do you know about me?" he asked, tamping down his anger. He didn't remember whether or not they'd talked about his background ten years ago.

"I know your parents were killed in an automobile accident and your grandfather took you in when you were fifteen. You were angry and rebellious and got into trouble with the sheriff a couple times during high school. Big trouble that made the newspapers. Very public stuff—''

''I'm sorry I asked.'' He turned left into the Dairy Queen driveway. There were only a couple of cars in the lot. ''Anything?''

''I don't see his car. I'll run inside and ask if anyone has seen him.''

Max watched her walk up to the door, then disappear inside. He didn't remember her being so skeptical, cynical and suspicious. She also hadn't been so sassy, scrappy and sexy. But that was beside the point. Where did she get off judging him? Whatever happened to walking a mile in a man's wingtips before forming an opinion? Living with Bentley Caine hadn't been a bed of roses. Did she know what the old man had done to him? What had convinced Max he'd be better off anywhere but Sweet Spring?

Ashley was back moments later. After sliding into the car she said, ''He hasn't been here, but they'll let me know if he comes in.''

He waited for her to buckle up. After looking both ways, he eased out into noticeably heavier traffic. Quitting time in town. If he was smart, he would quit too. But this wasn't the first time he hadn't been smart enough to live up to his potential.

''Did you ever ask my grandfather why I left?''

''I didn't know him then. By the time I did, it wasn't important anymore.''

That's not what her tone said. She was taking something very personally. Two could play that game. ''For the record, I didn't desert anyone.''

''No?''

''No.''

"But you did leave town?"

"Of course I did," he snapped. "And I had good reason."

"But Sweet Spring was your home—"

"It's his home, not mine. In spite of everything he did, I got an education, including a master's degree. I found out I was good at saving failing corporations from the brink of disaster and started my own free-lance consulting business. I do what's necessary—reduce staff, consolidate, or sell off unprofitable businesses."

"A heart of gold," she murmured.

"My reputation as a business fixer is well known," he shot back. "I'm justifiably proud of my level of success, and I did it without his help."

"Obviously he did *something* for you. You said you owed him enough to see him."

"Yeah."

The vibes he was getting from her said she was dug in on the old man's side. So what did he care? He was no longer a kid who didn't know where he belonged. But it did stick in his craw that she was loyal to the man who hadn't been loyal to his own flesh and blood. Apparently she saw a side to his grandfather that Max had never glimpsed.

"Tiny's BBQ is up ahead," she said, pointing toward a sign sporting a pig and a cow, nose to nose.

Max steered the car into the lot and waited while Ashley went inside. She wasn't gone long.

"Nothing," she said, after sliding back into her seat.

"I'll call the house. Maybe there's news."

Max pulled his cell phone out and hit the programmed number. The housekeeper answered and said she hadn't seen Mr. Caine but would let Max know if his grandfather came home.

He slid the phone into his pocket. "It's time to bring in the big guns."

"The sheriff's office is just down the street," she said, reading his mind.

"So do you believe no news is good news like the sheriff said?" Ashley asked Max. "That Mr. Caine will probably turn up tomorrow?"

"Yeah. For now, leaving the looking to the professionals seems like the best thing to do." His mouth thinned to a straight line. "Although it's frustrating. By this time I figured I would be on a plane back to California."

Had it really been a decade since she'd stared wide-eyed at bad boy Max Caine in the company cafeteria? Sitting across from him again, Ashley felt an odd sense of déjà vu. Then, she'd been flattered by attention from charismatic Max Caine. But now that she knew his true colors, she wasn't sure why she'd agreed to his dinner invitation.

The waiter left their check and Max took it. She got the feeling the gesture was automatic. Dinner out with a woman was probably par for his course, but hers had been seriously lacking in men. She didn't think Max was her type, which was a relief. Although she wasn't sure she had a type.

She'd been too busy working her way through college to pay much attention to the male of the species. And given the disastrous romantic track record of the Gallagher women, which included her mother, her sister and herself, she'd been grateful for the too-busy schedule that had kept her from dating.

In the cloud that was her struggle for a business degree, not dating had been the only silver lining. All of her relationship experiences had been disastrous. For her, dinner out with a man was a prequel to perdition. This wasn't a date. There was no reason to hang around and make small talk. The check had arrived. She was ready to leave now.

But Max took a sip of his half-finished beer, then set the longneck on the table showing he was in no hurry to go.

"Why are you so loyal to my grandfather?" he asked.

"He's always been there for me."

"When no one else was?" His gaze never left hers.

"Why would you go there?" she asked, defensive because his remark had hit way too close to the mark.

He raised one broad shoulder in a casual shrug. "I don't know. Nine times out of ten someone will say 'he was there for me when no one else was.' I filled in the blank."

"I don't need you to fill in my blanks. In my experience, your grandfather is fair and caring." When he opened his mouth to say something she held up a finger to silence him. "And before you ask, I've got plenty of support—family support."

But this guy didn't know the first thing about what she shared with her mother and sister. There was no point in discussing the fact that her father was a leaver, just like Max.

She dragged a finger through the condensation on

her water glass, then met his gaze. ''And I'm concerned about my family.''

''What about them?''

''My mother and sister work at Caine Chocolate.''

''Are they in management, too?''

She shook her head. ''A college degree is a requirement, and I'm the first in the family to get one. Your grandfather created the position of manager of specialty and seasonal items just for me. He told me the idea came to him out of the blue on my birthday—'' She stopped because she was blathering like an idiot.

''When?'' Max asked.

''On my birthday. It's February twenty-ninth.''

''Leap year?''

She nodded. ''Jordan and Rachel, my two best friends, were born the same day. Because of the unusual date, our families kept in touch. Since we only have a birthday once every four years, we celebrate together. This year it was in New Orleans.''

''And that's when my grandfather came up with the idea?''

''Yes,'' she said, an odd feeling raising goose bumps on her arms. That was the night they'd recovered the tacky brass lamp, à la Aladdin. The grateful shop owner dressed like a gypsy, had insisted they each rub the lamp and make a wish. Hers had been money and power—not that she was going to share that with Max. He'd think she was crazy.

''Mr. Caine waited to announce my promotion until I had my degree in my hot little hand.'' Had her wish been granted with the promotion? No, that was too weird.

Max looked at her. ''After doing the math, it occurs

to me that it took you a while to get that important piece of paper. I know you're brighter than the average bear. I have to ask—what took you so long?''

''I had to work full time to pay for college and help out at home. That tends to slow down the process. But I'm determined to make up for lost time.''

''Well your promotion is a good start.'' He took a sip of beer. ''But I always suspected you were determined enough to take over the world.''

There would never be a better time to ask. ''Are you back to take over the company for your grandfather?''

''Why would you think that?''

''Obviously he isn't getting any younger. His health is fragile. You haven't been back until now. I just wondered if—''

''The buzzards were circling?'' he interrupted, a muscle contracting in his cheek.

''Actually—yes.''

''No.'' He met her gaze. ''I don't want or need Caine Chocolate. You have more ties to the company than me. In fact, I could ask you the same thing. Do you have your eye on taking it over?''

''There are a lot of people more qualified than me.''

''But you're the one who's making up for lost time.'' His eyes narrowed.

''If the opportunity presented itself, I wouldn't turn it down. But I respect the fact that it's a family-owned company. If you want to fill in some blanks, there's one.''

''Okay. But I don't understand why you're so hostile.''

It was too much to hope he hadn't noticed. Normally, she was able to hide her feelings. In fact, she was feeling bad about all the one-liners she'd lobbed his way. And why had she done it? A lot of years had passed since they'd talked and she'd developed a crush on him. Was that enough reason for her grudge? Was she that weird?

Or was it because he'd been her first crush? As hard as she'd tried, she hadn't been able to forget him, probably because he *had* been her first. So to speak. The second time she'd let herself care about a man, her bad choice had made her life more difficult than it had to be. But Max had been her first personal experience in the curse of the Gallagher women. He was the first to show her men leave.

And it didn't bother her anymore that he'd left her. It was the cavalier way he'd completely turned his back on his grandfather that fried her grits. "You think I'm hostile?"

"Come on, Ash. I'm a lot of things, but stupid isn't one of them."

"Okay. You want to know why? I'll tell you. It's your behavior."

"Excuse me, but I haven't seen you for ten years. What do you know about my behavior?"

"I know you walked away without looking back."

"Has anyone ever told you there are two sides to every story?"

"I'm aware of that. Let me point out that adversity doesn't build character, it reveals it. Your behavior revealed that when there's a bump in the road, you're the kind of person who walks away and never comes back. Instead of trying to work things out."

"There was nothing to work out."

Anger ballooned inside her. ‘‘If that’s true, why did he hire a detective to find you? Why did he follow your career and save every scrap of information he came across about you?’’

‘‘You’d have to ask him.’’

‘‘No, I don’t. Because actions speak louder than words,’’ she said. ‘‘The way he repeatedly contacted you about coming back. How profoundly hurt he was when you ignored his seventieth birthday party. He knew you received the invitation, by the way.’’

‘‘I was working.’’

‘‘That’s not good enough. And you didn’t bother to RSVP. You didn’t even contact him and lie about why you wouldn’t be there. You just ignored him.’’

He folded his arms over his chest. ‘‘Did it ever occur to you it was kinder that way?’’

‘‘No,’’ she said, and her voice shook.

His gaze narrowed as he studied her. ‘‘Are we only talking about the fact that I haven’t been back to see my grandfather?’’

‘‘Not entirely.’’ Not if she was honest.

‘‘Okay. Then you need to give me a little more information.’’

‘‘How about the fact that you stood me up?’’

‘‘What?’’ He frowned. ‘‘When?’’

Oh, swell. He didn’t even remember. Could this get worse? ‘‘Never mind. It’s not important. Let’s drop it.’’

‘‘Let’s not. You’re ticked off about something. Put it all on the table so I can defend myself.’’

She took a deep breath. ‘‘Before you left town, I was grounded for a month. The deal was I went from summer school to the chocolate factory so my mother could keep an eye on me while she was at work.''

''I remember.''

''You went out of your way to talk to me. Every day at lunch.'' The anticipation of seeing him had been the main reason she'd gotten up every morning during that time. ''You even promised me a post-punishment meal, somewhere other than the company cafeteria.''

''I did?''

''Yeah.'' Why hadn't she just agreed that her hostility was all about his grandfather? In this case, honesty was *not* the best policy. ''We had a date...I mean we'd agreed on a place and time to meet. You didn't show up. A couple days later it was all over town that you'd left.''

He leaned toward her and rested his forearms on the table. ''It slipped my mind. I'm sorry.''

''Me, too.'' Sorry that the memory could still bother her even a little.

''Did it ever occur to you that I might have had a good reason for leaving?''

''No. I was fourteen.''

''And now you're twenty-four. A grown-up. Isn't it possible something came up that took precedence over the plans I made with you?''

She looked at him, remembering. She'd waited hours on her front porch for him to pick her up as promised. Every time the phone had rung, she'd raced inside to see if it was him. But it never was. What was so important that he couldn't even call to let her know he wouldn't be there? It took a long time for her to grow up enough to see that she'd been nothing but a sappy dreamer, and he'd duped the dope. And now it didn't matter.

"Sure, it's possible," she said.

"Your sincerity is underwhelming." A muscle contracted in his jaw. "So I have to conclude that either you blow things out of all reasonable proportion. Or—"

She knew she was going to regret asking. "Or what?"

"I'm paying for what another guy did to you. Just a shot in the dark," he said shrugging.

And that was another shot too darn close to the mark, she thought. "You're not paying for anything. Speaking of which," she said, "what do I owe you for dinner?"

He put a credit card on the check and signaled the waiter. "Nothing. Better late than never. Consider it your post-punishment meal."

"Thank you." She stood up. "I have to go now."

She walked through the restaurant not much caring whether or not he followed. It was irritating to realize he could be right. Her animosity just might be out of proportion to his crime. Her inner child could be throwing an unwarranted melodramatic tantrum. So the best solution was to give her inner child a time-out.

She drew in a deep cleansing breath when the evening air hit her. The sun had set and a breeze cooled her cheeks. Behind her she heard the door to the restaurant whisper open. The hair at her nape prickled, and she knew Max stood there.

He stopped beside her, holding his suit jacket by

one finger after slinging it over his shoulder. ‘‘I’ll take you back to your car.’’

She nodded. ‘‘Thanks.’’

When she reached out to open the car door, his hand brushed hers as he grabbed the handle and let her inside. Why did he have to be a gentleman? Worse, why did she have to feel warmth and that tingle from his slight touch?

She wanted him to be bad to the bone. She needed him to have a sleazy rap sheet she could add to. So far, all she had on him was standing her up, leaving without saying goodbye and ignoring his grandfather. That was unforgivable. She couldn’t understand why he’d rebuffed the older man’s attempts to patch up their relationship. And seeing the soul-deep hurt on the face of the kindly man who’d been like a father to her made her angry.

They drove in silence to the company parking lot and Ashley directed him to her small compact in the far corner. He stopped the BMW beside it.

‘‘Ashley?’’

She opened the door. ‘‘What?’’

‘‘Are you going to look for him?’’

She didn’t need to ask who he meant. ‘‘Do you think it’s necessary?’’

‘‘I think the sheriff is probably right that he’ll turn up when he’s ready.’’

‘‘But?’’ she asked, feeling he had more to say.

‘‘I’m action-oriented. If there’s a problem, I fix it.’’

‘‘So what are you saying?’’

He raked a hand through his hair. ‘‘I guess I’m saying that it’s getting late. The professionals need to do their thing. But if there's no news by morning, I'm going to look again on my own."

She turned her head and met his gaze in the harsh overhead light. She thought she saw a flicker of something in the depths of his blue eyes. "You're concerned about him, aren't you?"

"Of course not."

"You're trying to pretend you don't care."

"That takes too much energy," he denied. "After I see him, I'm gone. The sooner he's found, the better."

"Okay." She slid out of the car, then rested her hand on the door to slam it. Hesitating, she caught her top lip between her teeth.

"Tomorrow is Saturday," he said, stating the obvious.

"Yes it is. Why?"

"If you're not doing anything, would you help me look for him?"

"Why?" she asked again.

"Because you know him. And I have a feeling you're going to do it anyway. We could pool our resources. Two heads are better than one." He smiled suddenly, and she felt the power of it all the way to her toes. "I'm staying at the estate."

"Thanks for the breaking news."

"If I don't call to let you know he's turned up, meet me there."

Against her better judgment she said, "Okay."

Chapter Three

The next morning, Ashley parked her little car in front of the Caines' impressive English Tudor-style house. Her heart pounded and she told herself it was all about her surroundings and not the prospect of seeing Max Caine's smile. She hadn't heard from him and that meant there'd been no word from the senior Mr. Caine. Concern trickled through her though she told herself there was no cause for it.

After sliding out of the car, she stared at the brick-lined steps leading to the double mahogany doors with beveled leaded glass ovals in the center of each.

"Motivation for higher education," she mumbled.

Ten years ago she'd been grounded for nearly flunking her first year in high school. She'd taken summer classes to repeat algebra and history. Every day on the way into town, her mother had driven her past the Caine estate and told her she could have a house like this if she worked hard and went to college. The visual aid was seriously effective in convincing Ashley to put her nose to the educational grindstone.

If not for her unfortunate brain seizure in her senior year, aka falling in love, at this moment she'd be well on her way to achieving her goals. Romance had convinced her never to give up anything for a man.

She rang the doorbell and waited. Several moments later her ring was answered. Max stood there in worn jeans that fit his lean waist, hips and thighs like a second skin and a biceps-hugging black T-shirt that made him look every inch the rebel she remembered. His exploits were legendary. Especially the cherry bomb in the gym bathroom, climbing in Rita Mae Whitmire's bedroom window while her father stood guard on the front porch, and letting the air out of Sheriff Kent's tires.

She swallowed. "Good morning."

"Hi. Come on in," he said, opening the door wider for her to precede him into the house.

"Any news on Mr. Caine?"

He shut the door and met her gaze. "I just got off the phone with the sheriff and he had nothing new to report. There have been no Bentley Caine sightings."

She let out the breath she'd been holding. "Okay. So what do we do?"

"Have you had breakfast?"

"I didn't have time—"

"Follow me," he said.

"But shouldn't we get to work looking for your grandfather?"

"We will. But I can get more searching out of you if you're fed. It won't take long."

"I'm fine. I never eat—" She stopped when it sank

in that he was ignoring her and she was talking to his retreating back. A nice one it was, too—broad shoulders, narrowing to a trim waist and a fine example of why women go gaga over a man's rear end.

She looked around as she went after him. Surprisingly, the inside of her dream house wasn't flashy, but homey and comfortable. And big, big, big. The family room, with its high-volume ceiling, featured a large area rug over the wood floor where a beige semicircular corner group sat in front of an imposing floor-to-fourteen-foot-ceiling river rock fireplace. The dining area was filled with an oak ball-and-claw-foot table, ten chairs and a matching buffet grandly holding a space against the wall.

The kitchen was large, really large. An island in the center had beige and black-flecked granite tops that coordinated with the rest of the counters. The refrigerator had a false front that matched the cupboard doors. A combined oven and microwave, with a gas cooktop beside it, were tucked seamlessly into the expanse.

"I've only seen the house from the outside," she said. "The inside is pretty incredible, too."

He glanced around. "I suppose."

"How could you leave it?"

One of his eyebrows lifted questioningly. "I believe you know why."

"I know what you told me, but I still don't understand why. Families fight. They work it out."

"Some don't."

"My family struggled with a budget for as long as I can remember. You were born to this and walked away. I just don't get it."

He took a mug from the cupboard and poured coffee into it, then handed it to her. "Milk or sugar?"

"Black's fine. Are you going to answer my question?"

"Why did I walk away?" He leaned against the counter and folded his arms over his broad, muscular chest. "Some things are more important than four walls, no matter how much square footage and luxury those walls encompass."

"Such as?"

"Loyalty and integrity."

Interesting choice of words. She remembered a younger, still cynical, and every bit as sexy version of this man who'd befriended a geeky, hostile teenage girl. Now, high-profile magazines often showed his chiseled features in photos with beautiful, powerful female executives on his arm. Which one was the real Max Caine?

"Loyalty?" she said, then sipped her coffee. "Your grandfather kept tabs on you. He told me when you got your master's degree. He shared news of the successes of your consulting business. And he told me he contacted you to try and mend fences."

She found that callous and unfeeling, at odds with the young man who'd given the time of day to a nerdy fourteen-year-old. And if he did, in fact, have the emotions of an ice cube, why was he back now? Was he telling the truth when he'd said he would only be there long enough to see his grandfather, then catch the first plane out?

"When someone takes a shot at you, it's not especially bright to give them another opportunity," he said.

A shot at him? What was he talking about? That implied he felt wronged. But— No. She wasn't going to do this. She refused to waste any more energy on Max. Since he'd turned up in her office yesterday, she'd spent way too much time analyzing his motivations. And that made her cranky, curious and cautious in equal parts.

"Okay. Obviously we're going to have to agree to disagree. The sooner we start looking for your grandfather, the better," she said. "If you insist on feeding me breakfast first, let's get it over with."

"What would you like?" he asked, his voice dropping to give the words the *im*proper tone of double entendre.

Her heart skipped and she was annoyed at her involuntary response to him. "Are you going to call the butler to whip something up?" she said, struggling to keep her own voice from slipping into breathlessness.

She wasn't used to this give-and-take between the sexes. Until last night's dinner with Max, it had been a very long time since she'd been alone with a good-looking man. Her focus on school to the exclusion of almost everything else might have been too narrow. All those college classes hadn't prepared her for social situations. But she suspected a plethora of social awareness still wouldn't have prepared her to deal with Max Caine.

"Actually," he said. "I'm pretty good at whipping up a few things."

She'd just bet he was. Flirtation. Seduction. Surrender. "Toast would be fine," she said. "And quick."

"I'll throw in some scrambled eggs. It won't take long, then we can get down to business."

As Max quickly and efficiently rustled up the appropriate ingredients and cooking utensils, Ashley watched him work. The island between them gave her the illusion of a safe personal space.

Until seeing Max again, she'd thought time and maturity had put into perspective the magnified disillusionment of a fourteen-year-old girl. She was a grown woman who still felt the pull of his magnetism all the way to her toes. It was impossible for her to ignore the way his muscles rippled beneath the snug, soft fabric of his T-shirt. Her stomach contracted at the sight of his sleeves tightening around his biceps with every movement of the spatula.

She blew out a discreet breath when he finished and set a plate of eggs and toast on the island in front of her. Holding out his hand, he indicated she should sit on one of the bar stools there.

He refilled the mug he'd been using and joined her, resting his forearms on the counter. "Obviously Bentley's important to you. Enough for you to give up your day off."

She scooped up a forkful of fluffy egg and slid it into her mouth. After chewing for several moments she said, "Like I said, he's always been there for me. He's been like a father."

"The father you never had?"

She didn't remember telling him that. "Why would you assume? Are you filling in the blanks again?"

"Something like that."

"It's even more than that," she said, not confirming or denying the truth of his words. "Mr. Caine has done a lot for me. How can I abandon him when he might need help?"

He studied her for several moments, then nodded. "Okay. I guess we have to agree that we'll never fully understand each other's motivation. And move on."

"Sounds like a plan."

He grabbed a piece of paper she hadn't noticed on the counter. "Speaking of plans, I've been thinking about the best way to go about this search. Someone needs to be here in case he shows up. Chip is going to—"

"Chip?"

"The butler," he said, the corners of his mouth turning up. He obviously realized that the name was completely at odds with the profession of gentleman's gentleman. "He's going to man the phone. Call hospitals and other places I've instructed him to contact. You and I will do the mobile portion of the search." He put the paper flat on the countertop and turned it so she could see it. "I've done a spreadsheet of places to look for him and the most efficient way to accomplish the task. I need you to look it over, think about any place I might have neglected to put down."

She bit into her toast and chewed. "I'm impressed."

"Okay." One corner of his mouth tilted up. "Why?"

"You've obviously spent a lot of time and energy on this. A spreadsheet, for goodness' sake. Is that characteristic of a man who doesn't care?"

"I live for spreadsheets. Logic and organization are what I do. Don't read anything into it."

"No? Isn't there the tiniest possibility that you're here to reestablish a relationship with your grandfather?"

He huffed out a breath. "Nope."

"Really?" She studied him. "There's not even a slight chance that you might need family after all?"

"I don't need anything from anyone, especially my grandfather."

"Okay." She finished off the other piece of toast, admitting to herself she felt better after eating.

"I'm only here because I'm between consulting jobs and have some time on my hands. And you called."

Max rested his elbows on the counter and leaned forward, observing her without a word. He'd wondered if his attraction to Ashley would evaporate. He got his answer when his gaze zeroed in on her, focusing on her mouth, the full softness of her lower lip and the tantalizing curves of the upper. Intensity simmered through him along with a heat that couldn't be explained by the summer weather. It picked up speed and power as it ricocheted through him like a fireball. He wanted to kiss her. Throw caution to the wind and give into temptation. See if she was as soft and tantalizing as she looked.

"How many square feet did you say these four walls encompass?" she asked.

He blinked and met her gaze. "I don't believe I said. But if memory serves, about seven thousand."

"Not enough," she mumbled.

"What?"

"I said time's up." She rested her fork on the empty plate. "We have to get out there and find Mr. Caine."

Footsteps, slow and heavy, sounded on the wood floor behind her. "I didn't know I was lost."

Max straightened and stared over Ashley's head.

His heart pounded as the years melted away and he became an uncertain boy facing his stern, unyielding guardian. Bentley Caine looked older, his face thinner and more creased than Max remembered. Had he shrunk? His memories were of a man as tall as a tree and twice as hard.

"Hello, Bentley," he said, forcing a casual tone.

Ashley slid off her stool and hurried over to him. "Are you all right, Mr. Caine?"

"I'm fine," he answered. "I'm surprised to see you, Max."

"Are you?"

Max thought the old man's voice was different. Time had stolen some of the vigor from his normally booming tones. His grandfather's hair was pure white now, not the salt-and-pepper shade he remembered. Bentley Caine had aged. There was a time when Max had thought nothing could touch the tough old man, not even the hands of time. At least his blue eyes still snapped with attitude.

"Yes. I thought it would be a waste of Ashley's time to call and ask you to come home."

"Not home," Max retorted. The old man had made it clear a decade ago this estate had never been his home. "I came back to town."

Bentley walked across the room and stopped on the other side of the island. He smiled. "It's good to see you, son."

"I'm not your son." He put his hands on his hips. "Where the hell have you been?"

"We've been so worried," Ashley added.

Max didn't look at her. "When I got to the hospital they told me you walked out."

"That I did." He sniffed. "Coffee smells good. Any left?"

Max poured him a cup and set it on the other side of the island where his grandfather had taken a seat.

The old man took a cautious sip of the steaming liquid. "Not as good as The Fast Lane, but it'll do." He smiled at Ashley, who stood beside him. "I stopped in there this morning and Sam Fisher said the two of you were looking for me yesterday. I came home as soon as I knew you were here."

"Why did you leave the hospital?" Ashley rested an elbow on the island as she studied him.

"'Angels of mercy' my backside. They're a bunch of damned idiots," he grumbled. "Kept telling me to rest then woke me up every fifteen minutes to poke, prod, or pour something down my throat. How's an old man supposed to get any rest under those conditions?"

"Where have you been?" Max demanded. "Why didn't you come home?"

"Went to a hotel where no one could find me. I didn't want to be bothered." A gleam crept into his eyes. "Although if I'd known you were here..."

Ashley sat on the bar stool beside his grandfather's. "I'm glad you're all right, Mr. C. But the doctor said you have to take it easy."

"How am I supposed to do that?" Bentley said. "Got a company to run and folks depending on me. I have to get back to work before things fall apart."

"You can't," she protested. "It's against doctor's orders. You need to take it easy and get your strength back."

The gleam mutated into a crafty expression. ‘‘I’ll stay home.’’

‘‘Good,’’ Ashley said, smiling at him.

Max braced himself. Bentley Caine was a sly fox. He wasn’t the only one who’d kept up on news. Ashley had said the fruit doesn’t fall far from the tree, but she was wrong. Max wasn’t anything like him.

Bentley took another sip of his coffee, then set the mug down. ‘‘I’ll take the time to rest before going back to work if my grandson will agree to run the business while I do.’’

Max stiffened. That was a classic Bentley move—getting his way and looking like a saint. He should have seen it coming and blamed Ashley for his mental lapse. She’d fogged up his radar. His senses had blurred when he couldn’t take his eyes off her mouth and his mind wouldn’t let go of the urge to kiss her. In her orange and yellow sundress with skimpy straps and all that red hair, she reminded him of a firecracker waiting for the right spark to set it off.

Max had been off balance when his grandfather had walked in. The crafty devil had seen an opportunity and taken it. ‘‘Ten years ago you didn’t trust me to sweep the floors. Why would you want me to run the company now?’’

‘‘Because you’re a Caine.’’

‘‘I was a Caine when you accused me of stealing the family chocolate recipe and selling it to our competitors.’’

Ashley’s gasp of surprise told him she hadn’t known the whole story. But he tore his gaze from her surprised face and looked at the old man. Hurt, disillusionment and anger crashed over Max like waves egged on by a storm. He hated that it felt too much as it had ten years ago.

Bentley sighed and shook his head. "By the time I found out who actually stole the formula, you'd left town."

"Why didn't you go see Max?" Ashley asked.

"It wouldn't have done any good." He smiled wanly, looking every one of his seventy-two years. "But now you're back. We can—"

Max slammed his palm on the counter and savored the stinging that reverberated all the way up his arm to his shoulder. "There is no *we.* And I need to get my head examined for coming back here. If you'd been in the hospital like a normal cardiac patient, I'd have paid my respects and been on the first plane back to California. That was the plan. But you had to disappear." He ran his fingers through his hair. "Now that I've seen you, I can go back to the original plan. I'm going to catch the next plane out."

"What will it take to get you to stay?" the old man asked.

He was about to say nothing could make him change his mind. Then Max made the mistake of looking in Ashley's direction. Pity was painted all over her face. He hated that. At the same time, all he wanted to do was pull her into his arms. What was that all about?

He was a success in his own right, in spite of the old man telling him he wouldn't amount to anything. It had taught him not to turn the other cheek or give someone another shot. He remembered his grandfather saying never show weakness, never admit you're wrong. Max wondered if that was why he'd come back, to hear Bentley Caine admit he'd made a mistake.

"How about an apology?" he said.

His grandfather sat up straighter and folded his arms over his chest. "I've said all I'm going to say."

"Me too," Max snapped.

He turned on his heel and walked to the front door, opened it and went outside. He jogged down the steps and stomped away from the house. Behind him he heard footsteps crunching on the cement drive and increased his pace.

"Max, stop."

Ashley hurried to catch up with him, and she wondered why she was bothering. Obviously he was behaving true to character. But she couldn't forget the haunted look on Max's face when he'd said he hadn't come home, just back to town. And when he'd bristled at his grandfather calling him "son," it reminded her that he'd lost his parents. She didn't even want to think about how that would feel. And then he'd been exiled from the only family he had left. She couldn't let him leave like this.

"Please stop, Max. My legs are really short and I can't keep up."

He didn't even turn around so she increased her pace. Why couldn't she just let him go? Was it because Max had been there for her during a rough spot in her life? Was that the reason she felt compelled to do something about the rift between the stubborn Caine men? Although she didn't have a clue what that something might be, right now she just needed to make him stop. Because if Max left, she was sure he would never come back again. Later she would think about why the idea of that bothered her enough to send her racing after him like this.

Halfway down the drive, she caught up with him. ''Max, please stop,'' she said, huffing and puffing beside him as she struggled to keep pace with his long-legged stride. ''These sandals weren't made for walking, let alone this kind of aerobic activity. And I need to talk to you. But that takes oxygen and I'm almost fresh out.''

He slowed, then came to a halt and looked at her. ''What?'' he snapped.

''You have to run the business.''

''Give me one good reason why I should.'' He glared at her.

''If you don't, your grandfather will insist on going back to work and it wouldn't be good for him.''

''How about a reason that isn't about him.''

''The employees.'' She drew in air. ''The town. Everyone relies on Caine Chocolate for work. If anything happens to the company, this place could turn into a ghost town. You have an obligation to the future of Sweet Spring.''

''That's a stretch.'' He rested his hands on his hips. ''Anyone can run the company. What about you?''

''I don't have the experience yet. And he hasn't groomed anyone to take his place. It would take a while to find someone with the right skills who's also willing to live in a small town like this.''

''Including me.''

''But you're a Caine. Caine Chocolate has been family owned and operated since its inception over eighty years ago. It was started by your great-grandfather and survived the Depression. You've got

Caine blood running through your veins. The least you can do is take over temporarily. It's not like you don't have the business background.''

''It's not like I owe him anything.''

''Where's your sense of pride?''

Ashley knew she was fighting a losing battle. She'd appealed to his spirit of community and generational continuity. All she had left was his sense of family and it appeared that well was dry.

''Look, Max, it's no secret that his health is fragile. At least stay long enough for him to build up his strength and get medical clearance from his cardiologist to return to work. Then he can figure out who will take over and direct the future of the company.''

He looked at her, blue eyes intense. ''That's more consideration than he gave me.''

Frustration swelled inside her. ''How can you turn your back on the only family you've got?'' She put her hand on his arm. The skin was warm to her touch and the muscles beneath her palm contracted, the strength harnessed. ''He needs you.''

''And I needed—'' He drove his fingers through his hair. ''Never mind.''

''I hate being right about this.'' She dropped her hand. ''Adversity reveals character. Yours is to take off. To turn your back. To look straight ahead and never mind who gets hurt.''

''You think calling me names will change my mind?''

''I was hoping. If that doesn't work, I'll think of something else. Maybe if you—''

He touched a finger to her lips, silencing her. ''I've

heard a rumor that redheads have a legendary temper. Do they have legendary tenacity as well?''

''A mother lode of perseverance.'' Had she gotten through to him?

''You're not going to give up, are you?''

''No.''

He glanced away, into the distance and a muscle contracted in his cheek. Finally, he met her gaze again. ''You win. I'll stay.''

Chapter Four

Ten years ago Max had wondered what it would feel like to sit in his grandfather's chair and run Caine Chocolate. He squared his shoulders and sank into the soft leather desk chair for the first time. The old man knew comfort if not his grandson.

It still surprised Max that he'd wound up in charge of the company when all he'd planned to do was see his grandfather and leave town again. He'd have thought being played this way would annoy him, but it didn't. His lack of annoyance probably had something to do with his own sense of duty mixed with a dash of dogged determination from one stubborn redhead.

This was a new role for him—running a business as opposed to dismantling it. He'd gone from ruthless corporate consultant to chocolate company CEO in the blink of two big brown eyes.

Why couldn't he say no to Ashley? It should have

been easy. She wasn't especially beautiful—although the dusting of freckles on her nose, the wild cloud of red curls around her face, and her curvy little figure were cute and growing on him.

He was intrigued by her sharp tongue and keen wit, obvious signs of her intelligence. But she was definitely not stunning. So why hadn't he kept on walking? He would probably never know the answer to that question. But now he was stuck. He'd given his word, and in spite of what the old man thought, it *was* gold. At least he'd had the presence of mind to state his terms. He would stay at the company until his grandfather was released by his doctor to go back to work. Or until Max had another consulting job.

So now he was temporarily in charge. And first things first. He needed to get up to speed on every aspect of the business and he needed to do that pretty darn fast. He'd scheduled a meeting after lunch to introduce himself to the manager of each department. He intended to use the morning for general orientation. A company tour was first on his agenda. And he knew just who he wanted for his guide.

The intercom on his desk buzzed and he pushed the button. ''Yes?''

''Miss Gallagher is here, Mr. Caine.''

''Send her in, Bernice.''

Moments later, the door opened and Ashley entered. ''You wanted to see me?''

He'd sent for her—boss to employee. But he had to admit he *did* want to see her—man to woman. ''Yes. I'd like you to show me around the place.''

''Okay. But—''

''What?''

''I've only been in management a month. Are you sure you wouldn't rather have one of the guys who's been in administration longer to do it?''

He gave her the once-over. Her conservative navy pin-striped suit and matching low-heeled shoes had management written all over them. This morning her hair was up and pulled away from her face, neat and professional. Day before yesterday on the estate driveway, with the breeze blowing the fiery locks around her cheeks and brushing her shoulders, it had been all he could do to keep from tangling his fingers in its wildness. He'd wondered if the strands were as warm and exciting as they looked.

Today all her flash and energy was camouflaged by the corporate uniform. Oddly enough, he missed it. But something told him she couldn't keep that alter ego hidden indefinitely.

''Max?'' she prompted, waving her hand to get his attention. ''Are you sure you want me? To be your guide, I mean?''

''Hmm? Oh, right. The tour.'' He stood up. ''You'll do.''

Casual words in spite of the fact he noticed the slight spike in his pulse rate and the need for a deep breath to slow it down again.

For the next hour and a half she walked him through the three separate buildings of Caine Chocolate—production in one and marketing, distribution and research and development in another. The third building had been added after he'd left and it housed administration offices.

Now they were standing in the second building, a two-story structure. His hands rested on his hips as he surveyed the employees who wouldn't meet his gaze. Hmm. What was that all about?

"Isn't that where the administration offices used to be?" he asked, glancing up at a glassed-in space on the second floor. Once upon a time the area had been partitioned into cubicles.

Ashley glanced in the direction he indicated. "That's right. When distribution was bursting at the seams, Mr. Caine decided to house administration separately and use the space down here to expand marketing. I was a supervisor here before my promotion when I moved into the other building."

He met her gaze. "It occurs to me that if my grandfather hadn't moved you up the corporate ladder, I wouldn't have seen you when I went looking for him."

She frowned. "I suppose that's true. This is a big place."

"I wonder if it isn't too big," he mused.

"What do you mean?"

"It's possible production has become unwieldy."

"Are you talking about cutting back?"

"Not necessarily. Sometimes restructuring is successful. I won't know until I see everything, then have a chance to look over the financial reports."

"You're only here temporarily. Is it wise to start making changes?" She looked startled, as if she hadn't meant to say that. "Sorry. Sometimes I speak before thinking it through."

"No problem. It's a valid question. The answer—it's the CEO's responsibility to make sure an operation is running as smoothly as possible. No matter how long or short his tenure. If there are ways to reduce overhead and maximize profit, they should be implemented.''

''But things have been running smoothly for a long time. Maybe status quo is best while you're here.''

''Not if we want to take the company public on the stock market.''

''It's family-owned,'' she said. ''I never heard your grandfather mention taking it public.''

''That doesn't mean it isn't something that should be considered for the health of the business.''

''Caine Chocolate has enjoyed a great deal of success for over eighty years. If it ain't broke, don't fix it.''

He looked at her, the flush that stained her cheeks. Her eyes flashed, and he found he liked shaking her up, stirring the legendary latent passion of a redhead.

''If don't fix it means doing nothing, then it's not an option.''

''Why do you care?''

Good question. His grandfather had played him like a fiddle to get him to stay. All he had to do was rest on his laurels and put out any fires that came up. But apparently he wasn't a rest-on-his-laurels kind of guy.

''It's not a matter of caring. I believe there's always room for improvement. Since I've got nothing better to do, I figure I'll do what I think is best. If that means making changes, then that's what I'll do. It takes an infusion of capital to do that. Earnings would increase.''

''I'm not sure about increasing. That's a delicate balance. Expansion that's too rapid can be a disaster.'' She tucked a loose strand of hair behind her ear. ''As long as a company sees profit, it seems to me that some things are more important than the bottom line.''

''Steady profit isn't enough. If a company isn't growing it's dying.'' He watched her carefully, the emotions crossing her expressive face. She disapproved of sweeping changes; he'd bet money on it. One thing was certain. If she was going to make up for lost time and climb the corporate ladder, she would need to perfect a poker face.

She stuck her hands in the pockets of her slacks. ''Growing a company involves introducing new products. Don't you agree?'' Annoyance gave way to a spark that lit her brown eyes, making them glow with excitement.

''Yes. The secret is to know what the public wants before they do.''

''That's what Mr. Caine always says.''

Inwardly, Max winced at her comment. The fact that he was quoting his grandfather didn't mean anything. He wasn't like the old man. The sentiment of the adage was nothing more than common sense.

''I'd like to show you some of the ideas we're working on in R&D for the specialty and seasonal line,'' she continued.

''Good. I'd like to see them.''

He followed her to the second floor. The square footage in the loft area was partitioned into cubicles. In one, an easel was set up.

Ashley stopped beside it. ''Here we have some of the selections in our Christmas line. It's hard to think about that when it's not even the Fourth of July yet, but you learn to think ahead.''

''Yes,'' he said. His gaze strayed to the wisps of

copper hair shimmering around her face like a sizzling firecracker. And the gleam in her eyes glowed bright as a sparkler.

"We've got chocolate suckers shaped like Santa Claus, reindeer and Christmas trees. Clear cellophane tied with holiday ribbon containing solid chocolate balls wrapped in red, green and gold. A little sleigh that the consumer can fill with their own favorites or some packaged with our top sellers."

She took off her suit coat and draped it over a chair. As she indicated each item on display, her white blouse shifted and pulled across her chest. The silky material, just this side of see-through, outlined her firm breasts and tucked into her slacks, accentuating her slender waist.

"Hmm," he said, noting his pulse spiking again.

Purely male appreciation poured through him as he studied the enticingly feminine way she filled out her corporate costume. He wasn't sure why he'd agreed to stick around except running the company was something to do until his next consulting job. And watching Ashley wasn't boring.

"Over here I've been working on some ideas for Valentine's day." She moved to a drafting table in the corner.

He followed in the wake of her subtle fragrance, the perfume drawing him like a magnet. There was nothing subtle about the heat that licked through him. A decade ago, he hadn't felt like that when he'd hung out with her. If it wasn't for the fact that he knew she was career driven, choosing her as a tour guide could have been hazardous to his long-term peace of mind.

But she was focused on her job. Where was the harm in focusing on her while he was in town?

She picked up a red mug. "We fill this with hearts and cupids, a functional item when the candy is gone. Here we have the same cellophane bags, this time with red and silver wrapping the chocolate. Square dark and light chocolates with sayings like 'I Love You, Be Mine, Hug Me, Kiss Me' on them."

He liked the sound of the last two, especially if Ashley was involved. "Impressive."

"It's my goal to do something special for each and every month. Even the ones without a big holiday theme."

"A challenge."

"I'm hoping to increase the advertising budget. And utilize the Internet. I haven't had a chance to talk to Mr. Caine about that yet."

"I'd say you just did."

She smiled and a tiny dimple materialized in her left cheek. "I suppose I did. But you know what I mean."

"Yeah. And I—"

Footsteps sounded behind them. "Hey, Ash, I thought you might be here."

Max turned around. Two redheads stood there, one in her mid to late forties and one younger, more in Ashley's age range. He'd have to be a moron not to see the resemblance between the three of them.

"Hey, you guys." She glanced at him. "This is Max Caine, Mr. Caine's grandson. Max, my mother Jean and my sister Colleen."

He walked over and shook hands with each of the women. "Nice to meet you."

"I remember you." Jean looked him over.

"The rebel or the ingrate?" He met her gaze, but almost felt Ashley's flinch. What the heck? Might as well get it out of the way.

"Neither," she answered. "I try not to judge people. Company gossip blew the incident out of proportion, but I figured you had your reasons for not coming back."

That was refreshing. He glanced at Ashley and waited for a smart remark. None came. Hmm. "So which department do you work in?" he asked.

Jean smiled. "I'm a supervisor in distribution. Colleen is an associate in marketing. She's very creative."

"I'm taking art classes in the evening. My baby sister inspired me to go for it, although I'm still trying to figure out what I want to be when I grow up," she added.

Ashley smiled. "She's so artistic and had a lot to do with some of the new packaging and fantastic eye appeal."

"Sounds like you two make a good team," Max said, glancing at the two of them.

"How does it feel to be back in the saddle, so to speak?" Jean asked.

"I was never *in* the saddle," he said, figuring she was talking about working for the company. "And I'm just here temporarily."

"Until his grandfather gets the okay from his doctor to come back to work," Ashley explained.

"I see." Colleen narrowed her gaze on him. "So you're not planning to stick around?"

"No," he said. "My real job is corporate consulting. I never stay in one place long."

"Where do you call home?" Colleen asked.

She was taller than Ashley. Normally, Max figured the taller the better. He liked women with legs that went on longer than a sleepless night. But when he looked down at Ashley, he found her fragile femininity appealing. It brought out a protective streak he hadn't known was there.

"I've got a condo in Los Angeles," he said. "But I'm not there much."

"Must be hard," Jean said. She folded her arms over her chest.

"I'm used to it. But every once in a while it would be nice to have a home-cooked meal."

Jean looked at Ashley and Max could have sworn she shook her head slightly. When he met her gaze she gave him a small smile.

Her mother said, "How about tonight?"

"Excuse me?" he said.

"Why don't you come over to the house tonight and I'll fix you a home-cooked meal?"

"Okay."

"Good," Jean said. "Ashley can give you directions. We'll see you about seven."

Max watched them leave. Then he looked at Ashley. "You don't mind, do you?"

"Of course not."

If that was the truth, then why was the pulse at the base of her throat fluttering like the wings of a trapped butterfly? He would bet his last dime she'd wanted him to decline, even though she hadn't lobbed a verbal zinger his way since he became her temporary boss. Was she going soft? Inside as well as out?

As he watched Ashley put on the pin-striped jacket,

he wondered if she was really all work and no play. He knew she was a career-minded woman. His favorite—the kind who didn't have the time or the inclination for a relationship. Maybe he could coax her into a short-term association that didn't involve a long term commitment. That was why he'd accepted the dinner invitation.

She could be an appealing diversion while he was stuck in Sweet Spring. Besides, spending time with her and her family would be a better alternative than sitting across a dining room table from his grandfather.

Ashley knew Max was on the front step even before she heard the doorbell. Her heart had stuttered the moment she'd heard the car door slam. He was right on time. What had possessed him to accept an invitation to dine with the peons? He'd made it clear he wasn't there for the long haul, so this couldn't be about any sort of employer-employee bonding. What was his angle? And he must have one. Guys like him didn't hang out with people like them.

The bell rang again and her mother called out, "Ash? Can you get the door?"

"Okay," she answered.

Her mother and sister were in the kitchen fussing over dinner. She, on the other hand, was just fussing. Trying to get her I-don't-give-a-fig face in place for an evening with her temporary boss. But clearly that wasn't going to happen—the composure as opposed to the evening.

She brushed her hands over the hips of her denim shorts and checked to make sure her sleeveless white cotton blouse was neatly tucked into the waistband.

Since she was on her own turf, she'd decided to dress down. There was no need to impress him. She was on her own time and didn't care what he thought.

''Here goes nothing,'' she muttered, opening the door. She'd been taught not to be deliberately rude so she plastered a smile on her face. ''Hi, Max. Come in.''

''Ashley.''

He walked past her and looked around. Was he comparing their thirteen hundred square feet of the American dream to his family's estate? She glanced around the big oblong area that served as their living and dining room. The walls were painted mauve below the white chair rail. Above it was a floral wallpaper border in shades of pink, yellow and green. The corner fireplace was Ashley's favorite thing about the entire house, the only item that wasn't square, oblong and boring. Some day she was going to buy her mother a brand-new house with a great kitchen and lots of space.

''Nice place,'' he said.

''It's small. But we like it.''

He looked at the clay pot beside the door holding a dried flower arrangement. ''Very...pink.''

''What do you expect in a house with three women?''

His mouth turned up. ''Good point.''

''Mom and Colleen are in the kitchen. Dinner will be ready soon. Have a seat,'' she said, extending her hand to indicate the sofa.

''Thanks.''

He sat on the love seat her sister had recently re-covered. Instead of looking out of place or decreasing his masculinity, the froufrou, chenille-fashioned flowers only enhanced his appeal. He looked bigger, broader and more manly. His navy collared sport shirt tucked into tan slacks made his washboard stomach look even more washboardy. The shade brought out the blue in his unforgettable blue eyes. And when he leaned forward and rested his elbows on his knees the pose added more masculinity than she'd seen in a month of Sundays and sent her temperature skyrocketing. If you can't stand the heat, go into the kitchen.

"Can I get you something to drink?" she asked.

"No thanks." His gaze went to the doorway behind her and he stood up.

"Mr. Caine," her mother said.

Ashley turned as Jean and Colleen walked into the room.

"Mrs. Gallagher."

"Please, it's Jean."

He nodded. "If you'll call me Max."

"Max it is. Dinner's ready. I made lasagna," she said. "And I hope you're hungry."

"Sounds great. And I'm starving."

Ashley could have sworn he was looking at her mouth when he said that. Even though she must have been mistaken, her heart started pounding.

She took a deep breath. "Mom makes the best lasagna ever."

"Hi, Mr. Caine." Colleen put a steaming casserole on the dining room table.

"It's Max."

"Okay." She smiled. "I'll get the salad and bread."

"Sit anywhere," Ashley told him. "Mom, is there anything I can do to help?"

"No. Just sit."

But he didn't sit. He waited for her to and when she moved to her place, he held the chair for her. There was that gentleman thing again. Darned annoying. Especially since she'd learned he had a good reason for standing her up. A family squabble would tend to make a guy forget something like a kid's post-punishment meal. Now she could only hold against him the fact that he'd made it clear he wouldn't stay. That put him one step up from a guy who left without warning. It was up to her to crush any attraction or suffer the consequences. If only he looked like a troll and acted like a yahoo.

When everyone was seated, Jean served slices of lasagna and passed the plates to everyone, followed by salad and the bread basket.

Max sniffed. "This smells great."

"Mom makes the best vegetarian lasagna you've ever tasted," Colleen said.

Max glanced up. "Vegetarian?"

"You won't even miss the meat," Ashley assured him, struggling to suppress a grin.

"No meat," he said, staring at the square on his plate.

"What do you expect in a no testosterone zone?" Ashley said.

"It's been a long time since we had a man for dinner," Jean explained.

"Should I be afraid?" Max smiled his most charming smile.

Jean laughed. "That didn't come out right."

Colleen spread butter on her warm bread. ''What Mom meant is that we don't often have a man join us for dinner.''

''Speaking for the male population,'' he said, ''It's their loss.''

Silver-tongued devil, Ashley thought. When he met her gaze, she smiled sweetly. ''How nice,'' she said.

His right eyebrow rose questioningly. ''Is there any particular reason I'm the first in a long time?''

''Yes,'' Jean said. ''The Gallagher women are cursed.''

''Excuse me?'' Max's other eyebrow rose.

''It's true,'' Colleen confirmed.

''I started the tradition.'' Her mother chewed thoughtfully. ''My parents disowned me when I eloped with the girls' father. They didn't like him.'' She sighed. ''Turns out they were right. He left after I got pregnant with Ashley. Never saw him again.''

Ashley was squirming. There must be something to talk about besides ghastly Gallagher romantic karma. But she didn't know how to redirect the conversation without embarrassing her mother. That was something she would never do.

''Surely he helped financially,'' Max said.

Jean shook her head. ''He didn't want to be here of his own free will. So I didn't want anything from him. I took care of the girls just fine by myself.''

''I can see that,'' Max agreed. ''But you should have tracked him down and made him pay.''

''Maybe it would have set a better example for the girls if I had. Because Colleen was next. She was planning to go to Hollywood. Since she was a little girl she dreamed of a career in the movies or on TV. Saved as much as she could from her job at the company.''

''What happened?'' Max asked.

Ashley winced at the gravel in his voice. A slight frown appeared on his forehead. But she couldn't believe he was sincerely interested in this.

''Mom,'' Colleen said. ''Max doesn't need to hear the details.''

''He wouldn't have asked if he wasn't interested.'' Jean met his gaze. ''She met a rodeo rider. He said he loved her and wanted to take care of her. Sweet-talked her right out of her nest egg, then disappeared.''

Max's frown deepened. ''I don't know what to say,'' he admitted.

Colleen smiled. ''I'm over him.''

''You're a Gallagher woman,'' he said, looking at Ashley. ''If I didn't say it before, I will now. I'm deeply sorry about standing you up ten years ago.''

Ashley shook her head. ''That's history. Now I understand why. If I didn't say it before, I'll say it now, I forgive you.''

''So I wasn't part of the curse?'' When she shook her head, he asked, ''Who was?''

''That would be Tobey Tanner,'' Jean said. ''He was a good-looking, featherheaded—''

''Mom,'' Ashley said sharply, meeting her mother's gaze. This whole conversation was humiliating. ''I'd rather forget about that.''

''Share and share alike,'' Colleen said. ''If we couldn't forget my foolishness, why should you get off the hook?''

''Because you don't mind and I do,'' Ashley said.

Max put down his fork. "I don't want anyone to be uncomfortable."

That surprised her. How awfully darned sensitive of him. And that sort of tended to get a girl to lower her guard. She met his gaze. "All I'll say is that in the grand tradition of the Gallagher women, I gave up something for a man who left."

"What—"

"Forget it," she said. "What part of 'all I'll say' did you not understand?"

"Wow, sis," Colleen said. "Way to talk back to the boss."

Max shook his head. "Not tonight. I'm a guest in your home."

"It wouldn't matter if you were the president of the United States," Jean said. "She won't tell you any more. Ash is stubborn. More lasagna anyone?" When everyone declined, she stood. "If you'll pass your plates this way, I'll clear and bring out dessert."

"I'll help, Mom," Colleen said.

Ashley stood. "Me, too."

"That's okay, sis. We can handle it. You keep Max company." Colleen winked.

When they were alone, Ashley looked at him. "I'm sorry you had to sit through all of that. And with vegetarian lasagna no less. Not even a slab of manly red meat to take the edge off."

He grinned. "It wasn't that bad."

"It was like a bad country and western song."

"On the contrary, it was interesting." At her oh-puh-leeze look, he grinned and said, "At least now I understand all the pink."

"What's to understand? Pink is a color not a psychological commentary."

"If you say so." His smile faded. "Were you telling the truth? Was I part of the curse when I stood you up?"

"Of course not," she answered automatically.

But the truth was, he'd been the first to contribute to her quota. She understood why, but that didn't help much, because she'd been dumped on a second time. There wouldn't be a third.

"Families," he said, shaking his head. "Can't live with 'em. Can't drag 'em behind the camper."

"What do you know about families?" she asked.

"Well, I—"

"Let's get one thing straight." She leaned her elbows on the table and rested her chin on her linked fingers. "I'm the only one allowed to pick on my mother and sister. They've always been there for me. Unlike men who come and go."

"Funny," he said, looking not in the least put out. "In my experience, family comes and goes."

Her pique disappeared and her conscience kicked in when she wondered if he was remembering how it had felt to lose his parents. "Sorry, Max. I guess I climbed up on my soapbox. But I'm kind of protective. Take it from me, family dynamics require that you meet your relatives halfway."

"I'll keep that in mind."

For how long, she wondered, studying his handsome face. She gave him points for coming back when his grandfather got sick. And he'd stayed—albeit after some serious arm-twisting and guilt-tripping. But she believed that a leopard didn't change its spots, and she wouldn't put it past him to walk out again without warning.

She would keep *that* uppermost in her mind.

Chapter Five

Ashley hit the line two button on the phone and said into the receiver, "Ashley Gallagher. May I help you?"

"I hope so," answered a familiar gruff voice on the other end.

"Hi, Mr. C." She was genuinely pleased to hear from the older man. "How are you feeling?"

"About as useful as an ice cube tray in hell."

"Good. That means you're following doctor's orders to rest and take care of yourself."

"Humpf."

She smiled. As intimidation, this crotchety act had worked for about five seconds. She knew from personal experience that his heart was as soft as caramel beneath the crispy chocolate coating.

"What can I do for you, sir?"

"You can tell me how my grandson is getting along there."

"Everything is running smoothly."

Except her heart. Any mention of Max always seemed to make her ticker skip a beat or two and she worked hard at not being a casualty of his good looks and smooth charm.

"I'm not talking about the company. I mean is he causing trouble? He's been there two weeks. Is he making everyone want to quit? Or, is he making friends? Does everyone like him? Hell, forget everyone. Does *anyone* like him? No one knows better than me how he can be."

She knew Max was living in the guest house on the estate while he was in town. But for goodness' sake, didn't the two stubborn men communicate at all, even on a superficial level?

"What does Max say?" she prodded.

"Not much." There was frustration. "Generalities like you just gave me. Nothing personal."

"If you want specific answers, sir, you need to ask specific questions."

"He'll think I'm prying into his life."

"He would be right," she said, leaning back in her chair. "Why don't you ask him straight out what you want to know?"

"Already have."

"And?"

"Damn generalities. Said everything's fine. I shouldn't worry. That boy is smoother than a butter cream truffle."

Didn't she know it. Either Max still had issues with his grandfather and was giving him the cold shoulder. Or his refusal to discuss the company meant he cared enough to protect the older man from the stress and pressure of running it.

''He's right, sir. Don't worry. Everything *is* fine.''

Including the fact that she'd been able to deflect Max. That evening at her house had opened the invitation door. For drinks. Or dinner and a movie. She'd managed to dodge a couple. Accepting would be like walking naked in a hailstorm.

''Fine? That's not good enough. I want to know details,'' the elder Mr. Caine said.

''Did you ask Max for details?''

''Yeah. He changed the subject.'' A gusty sigh came loud and clear over the line. ''I want him to feel like one of the team.''

Then she wasn't going to burst his bubble by telling the elder Mr. Caine that Max interacted with the employees as little as possible. That he had lunch at his desk or went out instead of eating in the cafeteria.

''I'm sure he does, sir.''

''Horse pucky. He never goes out—not since the night he had dinner at your house. Nice of Jean to invite him, by the way,'' he mumbled.

''It was our pleasure, sir.''

In her dictionary, ''never goes out'' translated to ''no female companionship.'' God help her, she couldn't keep from smiling. It was shallow and selfish to be pleased about his lack of a social life, but she couldn't control the zing of satisfaction that shot through her. Then a thought surfaced.

''Sir, how do you know he doesn't go out? I thought he was staying in the guest house. Are you spying on him?''

''That's not important. Point is he's a young man with… Never mind.''

''I get your drift, Mr. C.''

''Do you? I saw this TV psychiatrist talking about what happens if needs aren't met. It's not pretty, Ashley.''

''I'm sure it's not, sir. Maybe you should watch old movies instead.''

''The point is, it's important to me that he fit in there at CCC.''

''I don't mean to offend you, sir, but this is very middle-school-parent if you know what I mean.''

''I do. And your point is?''

''He made it clear that his time at the company is temporary.''

''Doesn't mean the time he spends here shouldn't be pleasant.''

''That's true, sir.'' Now it was her turn to sigh. ''But if he's not inclined to reach out in friendship, there's not much you can do.'' She wasn't going to share that Max had reached out to her. The younger Mr. Caine had picked the wrong woman to try and fit in with. The silence on the other end of the line gave her pause. ''Mr. Caine? Are you still there?''

He cleared his throat. ''It's obvious the boy won't listen to me. When I try to get personal he makes polite but meaningless conversation about politics and the weather. And you know as well as I do that Texas summers don't yield much to talk about. Hot and humid, continued hot and humid. Doesn't cool off at night, just gets dark,'' he grumbled.

''At least you're talking to each other,'' she said,

piling her tone with all the positive perkiness she could manage.

"Humpf." He coughed. "You're right about one thing. Some things don't change. He wouldn't listen to me when he was a boy and he won't listen now. So I can't do anything. But maybe there's something you can do."

Oh, no. Did Max tell him he'd asked her out? Of course not. The two of them were exchanging little more than idle conversation. "What's that, sir? Just name it and I'd be happy to give it a try. If possible," she added for wiggle room. Because going out with Max Caine wasn't possible.

"Do you remember the welcome reception we had for Bernice when she first came to CCC? You should. It was your idea."

"Yes, sir, I remember." She'd suggested it to him after taking a business class. The theory being that employees who become friendly and bond as a cohesive unit will be more productive. They're more likely to pick up the slack for each other and the day-to-day business operations run more smoothly.

"Why don't you do that for Max?" he suggested.

She didn't want to get involved with Max in anything that wasn't strictly about work—meaning budgets, marketing and spreadsheets. That last thought generated the unexpected vision in her mind of twisted percale and intertwined bodies. Since when were spreadsheets a sexy thought? Since Max Caine came back to town. This was really bad.

"Sir, do you really think that's a good idea?"

"It's my idea. 'Course I think it's good."

It was on the tip of her tongue to suggest he ask

Bernice to organize something. But she knew he would say if he'd wanted Bernice to do it, he'd have asked her. And Ashley had heard the edge to his voice and hoped he wasn't getting himself worked up. He was supposed to stay calm. Heaven forbid he have a setback. Max could be here longer. No way. She wouldn't have any peace of mind until he was gone. The sooner Bentley was back on his feet and in control of his company, the sooner her own life and sexy, traitorous thoughts could get back to normal. No matter how boring and chaste that might be.

"A welcome reception is a great idea, sir. I wish I'd thought of it. I'll put something together. Would you like to come?"

"No."

"I'm sorry to hear that."

He cleared his throat. "I don't want to rock the boat. The two of us are doing okay. But if I butt in…"

"I understand, sir. I'll do my best to make him feel welcome."

And keep her heart idling in neutral while Max was here.

Standing in the doorway, Ashley caught her breath after hurrying to the company cafeteria. She'd intended to get there early and make sure everything was ready for Max's reception. But she'd been delayed by a phone call. Looking at her watch, she realized she was right on time.

"Impressive turnout," she mumbled, glancing around the crowded cafeteria.

Her heart had not been in this. Max didn't want to be there—at the reception or at the company. She shared his sentiment; she didn't want him there, either. And, come to think of it, she didn't see him.

She greeted people as she threaded her way through circular tables surrounded by chrome and orange plastic chairs. Her objective was the buffet spread set against the wall where a line of people waited. Ashley noticed that there was a pretty good dent in the finger sandwiches, fruit, sliced vegetables, and pastries.

She walked up to a group of three—two men and a woman. "Have you guys seen Max—Mr. Caine?"

"I came in about fifteen minutes ago." Balding, bespectacled Ken Edens, who worked in the accounting department, shook his head. "He wasn't here."

Ashley searched the faces of the people milling around the cafeteria. Ten years ago she'd been looking for the same man in the same place. "I may have to go find him."

"Whatever blows your skirt off." Cherry Addison nibbled on a celery stick.

Ashley looked at the tall, skinny brunette. The words "skirt" and "off" should never be used in connection with Max Caine. "What do you guys think of him?"

Greg Karlik met her gaze. "Permission to speak freely."

Ashley smiled. The dark-haired, ramrod straight man was retired military, but old habits died hard. He wasn't tall, only about four or five inches above her own five feet three.

"Of course," she said.

"He's a hands-on type."

Ashley shivered involuntarily. Business not personal, she reminded herself.

Ken looked around. ‘‘But the majority of CCC rank and file are wary of that.’’

‘‘Why?’’ Ashley asked.

‘‘Because,’’ Cherry said, ‘‘we don’t want him messing with things.’’

‘‘The least you could do is meet him halfway,’’ Ashley argued.

‘‘Why?’’ Ken said. ‘‘Based on his history it’s not worth the effort.’’

‘‘There’s something you should know about Max. He left town after a family argument. His grandfather had something to do with it. And you know how stubborn he can be.’’

‘‘So?’’ Cherry shrugged. ‘‘It’s common knowledge that the old man had a change of heart and tried to get him to come home. Max ignored him.’’

‘‘But he’s not doing that now. Shouldn’t we let bygones be bygones?’’

‘‘The prodigal son returns?’’ Ken wore a disapproving look.

‘‘That. And your boss, his grandfather, wants him here,’’ Ashley pointed out.

‘‘He’s an ingrate,’’ Greg said. ‘‘Old man Caine tried to make amends and the kid rebuffed them. He has no loyalty to his own flesh and blood. We’re just small cogs in the company wheel. Why should we trust someone like that?’’

‘‘Besides,’’ Cherry said. ‘‘He’s like a substitute teacher. Maintain order and stability, but no big changes. Why should we put ourselves out? He won’t be here that long.’’

Ashley’s heart skipped at the words. She thought again how she hadn’t seen him all day. ‘‘You should put yourselves out in the interest of common courtesy. You should welcome him out of loyalty to his grandfather.''

''Loyalty is earned,'' Ken pointed out.

Cherry rested her hand on her hip. ''And might I point out that he didn't bother to show up at this little get-together. We're here.''

''You just came for the free food,'' Ashley said.

Greg lifted one shoulder in a shrug. ''I don't dispute that. But where is he?''

Good question, Ashley thought. She glanced at the doorway. Speaking of the devil. Relief or something closely resembling it washed through her. In one of those moments of absolute clarity, she realized she wondered every day if that would be the day he was gone without a word.

''Max,'' she called out, smiling brightly. ''Come join us.'' She narrowed her gaze on her three companions. ''You guys need to adjust your attitudes,'' she whispered.

''I like my attitude,'' Cherry defended.

''Let me rephrase. Keep an open mind where Max Caine is concerned.''

Greg nodded seriously. ''We'll think about keeping an open mind regarding the younger Mr. Caine.''

''You guys are hopeless,'' Ashley whispered.

''Thank you,'' Ken said, pushing his glasses up on his nose.

''He's coming over. Give him a hearty Sweet Spring, Texas, welcome.''

When Max joined them, Ashley reminded him who everyone was. ''Do you remember Greg? He's in distribution. Ken runs the accounting department. And Cherry is in charge of marketing.''

''I remember,'' Max answered.

The three CCC employees stared at him and he looked calmly back. But no one made any attempt at conversation. Could this be more awkward? Ashley groaned inwardly. It had been much easier with Bernice.

''Anyone have big plans this weekend?'' she asked. Shrugs and mumbles were her only reply. Max didn't bother to shrug or mumble. He merely stared at her with a shuttered expression, until traces of amusement leaked through. He was getting a kick out of her discomfort. ''How about you, Max? Anything going on?''

''No.''

''Ken,'' she said, shifting to avoid the glare coming through the window and reflecting off his wire-rimmed spectacles. ''Don't you have a place at the lake?''

''Yes.''

She sighed. ''Do you use it much?''

''Yes.''

''I thought you had a boat. Any water skiing?''

''Some,'' he said, shifting his feet.

This was excruciating. She looked around the room and noticed the other people talking amongst themselves. She longed to be with them, but she'd promised Mr. C.

''Cherry, how's the family?'' she asked.

''Good.'' She looked at the watch on her stick-thin wrist. ''In fact, I have to go. Kids. Day care,'' she said vaguely, shrugging at Max.

The men mumbled something about leaving and en

masse the three set their plates on the buffet table, said goodbye, and left.

Ashley dragged Max from group to group, making sure everyone had an opportunity to say hello. People were polite, but cool. Not the rousing success Mr. C. envisioned.

''Nice party,'' Max said, when the place was nearly empty.

Ashley met his sardonic gaze. ''Thanks.''

''Nice turnout. How much did you bribe them to come?''

She sighed. ''Look, Max—''

''It was pretty clear they'd rather be having root canals.'' When she opened her mouth to deny it, he held up his hand. ''And I don't blame them.''

Ashley had arranged for the cafeteria staff to clean up. Together she and Max walked out and back to his office. Bernice had left for the day, but her work area was tidy. Max leaned a hip against her desk as he looked at Ashley. His red and navy blue silk tie was at half-mast. The sleeves of his dress shirt were rolled to just above his elbows, the image of the busy executive. The image of the sexy executive. She let out a long breath.

''Shake it off, Ash.''

Should she tell him it was his grandfather's idea? Something told her that idea wasn't any better than throwing a reception for a loner CEO. She let out another long breath.

''Would it help if I said I appreciate the effort?''

Effort being the operative word. She'd never worked so hard in her life as she had while trying to start conversations between people who didn't want to talk. And he hadn't been any help. Monosyllabic responses didn't a conversation make.

"Not much. You didn't make any attempt to bond with the employees," she pointed out. "In fact you hung me out to dry."

"It looked to me like Ken, Cherry and Greg were doing that for me."

"You could have jumped in to help any time," she said.

"I'm getting the distinct impression that you feel I'm somehow to blame. Care to elaborate?"

He folded his arms over his chest. To say the least, it made him a pretty impressive sight. The wrinkled white shirt made his chest look even broader. His hair was disheveled, as if he'd run his fingers through it countless times during the day. The navy slacks were creased from sitting behind his desk for hours. What was it about this rumpled executive look that made her heart speed up? Very deliberately, she stayed a foot away from him.

"You really are a gunslinger, you know that?"

One of his sandy eyebrows lifted. "Define gunslinger?"

"A loner. Rides in, gets the job done, rides out. Doesn't play well with others."

"Hmm." He grinned. "I like the sound of that."

"It wasn't a compliment." She rested her hands on her hips and watched his gaze drop, followed by a gleam in his eyes.

"Want to come into my office and sit down?" he invited.

She shook her head. "Feels good to stand."

"Okay. I guess it's better to stand on your soapbox while you make this my fault."

"It was merely an observation."

"An observation with the subtext that the fact people didn't have a good time is somehow my fault. I told you it wasn't a good idea."

"It was. While you're stuck here at CCC, what's wrong with making the best of it?"

"I thought I was doing that. But apparently you have a different take. I'm going to be sorry for asking, but what is it you think I should be doing?"

"Bond with your employees." Because your grandfather wants you to be happy here, she wanted to say.

"Bond?"

"Yes."

"I don't do bonding," he stated flatly.

"Have you ever tried? Certainly not since you've been here." She met his gaze.

"How do you know?"

"Bernice shared your general schedule during the day."

"Ah," he said nodding.

"Sincerity is half the battle, Max."

"I have been sincerely keeping to myself."

"And that screams insincerity. You've been gone a long time, but you can't have completely forgotten. These people can spot the lack of sincerity a mile away."

"Is that so?"

"Yes." She tapped her lip. "There are courses you could take."

"Such as?"

"Social interaction with employees. Tips for managers. Catch them doing something right. Recognize a problem exists. Talk to clear the air. Charm school. Attila the Hun's business etiquette for dummies.''

One corner of his mouth lifted. ''Why should I bother?''

''Because they'll come around if you make the first move and meet them halfway.''

''I'm here to do a job. Not win a popularity contest. So, again I say—why should I bother?''

''Just…because,'' she said lamely.

''Ash, I'm filler until the old man comes back. Until then my only function is to keep things from falling apart. There's no reason to waste energy on bonding.''

That's what Cherry had said and they were both right. But that wasn't going to make his grandfather happy.

She sighed. ''I guess I can understand your point.''

''Speaking of points, it's obvious I didn't make any with you.''

She stared at his mouth. He would if he kissed her, she thought. She must be losing her mind.

''I guess I thought you might have a change of heart and stay for the long haul. To help out your grandfather,'' she admitted. Another one of those moments of crystal clarity.

He shook his head. ''I don't do the long haul. Not the code of the road for gunslingers.''

''Yeah. I guess I knew that.''

''What if I told you I think my grandfather would be better off selling the business?''

That stunned her. ''You're joking.''

''Do I look like I'm joking?'' He studied her. ''A word of advice—you should work on developing a poker face. Everything you're feeling shows, and it's not a good thing in the business world."

"So noted." She shook her head. "I'll work on it tomorrow. Right now I have to say that I don't think your grandfather would agree with you. Obviously your heart's not in this company. And I've seen no overt affection for your grandfather. So, I have to ask. Why did you agree to stay in the first place?"

"Because of you."

"Me?" Oh, Lord. What did she do with that information? Deflect him with humor. Then—run far, run fast. "That was a good one. You had me for a second. I have to go, Max."

"Any chance I can talk you into going out to dinner with me?"

Now that was an idea she knew was bad. And if his grandfather ever found out she felt that way, he wouldn't be happy.

"Sorry. I've got plans."

He lifted a broad shoulder. "Maybe another time."

Maybe when hell freezes over. "See you."

"Have a good evening."

She walked out of his office. She needed to spend this evening and every other one until the senior Mr. Caine came back to work reminding herself not to feel anything personal for Max Caine. Professional only. Poker face, just like he'd said. Because if he could see how much she wanted him to kiss her, any gunslinger worth his salt would use it to his advantage.

Until Mr. C. returned and things got back to normal, her goal was to give Max Caine zero advantage.

Chapter Six

Ashley walked into The Fast Lane and looked around. She spotted Bentley Caine in a corner booth talking to Sally Jean Simmons, the waitress.

She walked past several occupied booths to where he was sitting. "Hello, sir. Sally Jean."

"Hey, there, Ashley." She smiled and put two menus on the gray Formica table. "What can I get you to drink?"

"Iced tea," he said to the tall, attractive, green-eyed brunette.

Ashley slid into the red-tufted Naugahyde bench seat across from him. "Me, too. And I'd like the Cobb salad. Save you a trip."

"Make it two. Sounds good to me." Mr. Caine shook his head and sighed. "Actually it doesn't. The fried chicken is calling to me, but I can't risk it." He winked at the waitress. "If it got back to my doctor, there would be hell to pay."

"Coming right up." The waitress hurried away.

Ashley studied the older man. It was good to see him. The last time had been when he'd turned up in his kitchen. "How are you feeling, sir?"

"The doctor says I'm making fine progress."

"Glad to hear it. You look wonderful. Rested and relaxed."

"Thank you. I feel pretty good, too."

"To what do I owe this lunch invitation?" she asked, curious about his motivation.

"Right to the point. I like that about you. Tell me how the reception went."

"Did you ask Max?" she hedged.

"Yes. He said it was fine." The last word put a scowl on his face.

"He's right, sir."

"Don't blow smoke up my—" He cleared his throat. "Fine tells me nothing. I want specifics." When she hesitated, he said, "Don't sugarcoat it for me, Ashley. And I don't need to hear that I'm behaving like a junior high dad. Just give me the facts."

She sighed. "All right. The cafeteria staff did an outstanding job on the food. The finger sandwiches were tasty as well as visually appealing. And I'm told the little pastries melted in your mouth—"

He held up his hand. "Ashley, you know that's not what I meant."

"All right," she said, unfolding her napkin-wrapped utensils and spreading them out on the table. "It didn't go quite as you'd hoped, sir."

"I was afraid of that. Why not? What happened?"

"A lot of people showed up."

"That's good." He studied her. "Isn't it?"

"It would have been, if he'd put some effort into making conversation."

"Look, I know I'm putting you in an awkward position. And believe me, I plan no repercussions to you or anyone else there at the company. I just need to know what's going on. And I trust you to give it to me straight."

"All right, sir." She let out a long breath. "The employees are wary and suspicious of him. He obviously doesn't have your flair as a people person."

"Are you flattering me, young woman?"

She smiled. "Is it working?"

He chuckled. "I'm ashamed to admit it is."

"About Max. Can you really blame them for not embracing him? They know he's only filling in for you. So why should they bother to make any kind of emotional investment?"

She was speaking for the rank and file of CCC, but the words were true for her, too. As far as emotional investments, Max was a very bad risk.

"I see," he said, a tinge of defeat in his tone.

"I'm sorry the report isn't better, Mr. C."

"Not your fault, my dear. You can lead a horse to water— And all of that."

"Right." Normally his voice boomed with energy and vigor. The lack of it bothered her. "Are you sure you're feeling all right?"

"I'd be feeling a lot better if people would stop asking me that."

She grinned. "It just means that we care about you. We're concerned about your health."

"It means everyone expected me to be pushing up daisies."

"Your spirited response gives me hope that won't be happening any time soon."

"Is that so?"

"Absolutely. We're looking forward to seeing you back at the helm soon, sir."

He sighed. "Thank you for trying, Ashley. With Max, I mean."

"You're welcome."

But she hadn't really tried. Oh, she'd tried to keep the conversation going—a bridge over troubled waters. But her heart hadn't been in it. Maybe everyone sensed that. Maybe if she'd sincerely welcomed Max. But she couldn't. She'd have to put her heart into it and that's something she couldn't do.

Except Mr. C. sounded so forlorn, she felt badly for him. But what was she supposed to do? She was counting the days until Max was gone. She looked forward to the day she would come to work *knowing* she wouldn't see him there. Not holding her breath wondering if he'd be gone without a word.

The sooner he was out of her life the better.

A week later, Ashley looked up to find her mother standing in her office doorway with Cherry Addison.

"Hi, Mom. Cherry."

"Are you busy, honey?"

"Nothing I can't stop. Come on in." She noted the frown on her mother's face. The other woman didn't look any happier. Ashley indicated the two chairs in front of her desk. "Have a seat. This is a nice surprise."

When they were settled, Jean nervously tucked a

strand of red hair behind her ear. ‘‘Surprise, yes. Nice? Not so much.’’

Ashley put down her pen. ‘‘What’s wrong?’’

‘‘Rumors,’’ Cherry said.

‘‘Rumors?’’ Ashley struggled to conceal a smile.

‘‘Yes. And don’t think I don’t know you’re trying not to laugh,’’ her mother said. ‘‘But trust me. This is really big.’’

‘‘How long have you worked for this company?’’ When her mother opened her mouth to answer, she said, ‘‘That was a rhetorical question. The point is, you should know by now that CCC rumors are like the *National Enquirer.* They should be taken with a grain of salt,’’ Ashley reminded her.

‘‘And like the *National Enquirer,* nine times out of ten scuttlebutt and gossip turns out to be true,’’ Cherry said. ‘‘Except for the alien abduction stories.’’

Ashley leaned back in her chair. ‘‘Rumors are usually nothing more than idle talk or an offhanded opinion widely disseminated with no discernible source. You can’t worry about every little thing you hear that may or may not be true.’’

‘‘And I don’t.’’ Jean shook her head. ‘‘This one would be no different if not for the fact that Bentley Caine had a heart attack. If it’s true, our jobs could be in jeopardy.’’

Although Jean Gallagher looked younger than her forty-seven years, the grooves marring the smooth skin of her forehead said she was worried. The fine lines around her blue eyes were from lots of laughter, but she wasn’t laughing now. She was really shook up about something. In general, she wasn’t an alarmist. And that got Ashley’s attention.

"What have you heard?" she asked, sitting up straight.

Cherry scooted forward. "I heard from Randy Donnelly in accounts receivable, who heard from Will Webster in production, who heard from Larry Evans in marketing that there's a good chance the company will be sold."

Ashley recalled Max saying that his grandfather would be better off if he sold the business. Was there actually a grain of truth in this rumor? Had he talked the older man into selling? "I see."

"I don't," her mother commented. "Profits are up. Business is good. Why would selling be an option?"

"Even if it's more than rumor—and I'm not saying it is—there's no reason to panic," Ashley pointed out.

"When would you suggest we panic?" Cherry asked.

"Before a sale or merger happens, there are about eight hundred things that have to fall into place and we're at maybe number ten."

"But what if it happens?" Cherry said.

Jean looked back and met her gaze. "Yeah. When companies merge, people always lose their jobs."

"Mom, really, I wish you wouldn't go to the bad place," Ashley said.

"There's no good place to go with this kind of information," she retorted. "And look at us. You and Colleen and me. We're all dependent on CCC for our livelihood. All our eggs in one basket. How smart is that?"

"Yeah," Cherry said. "And in this town, where else are you going to find a job? It's a one-company town unless you're in ranching."

Ashley knew she was right. She knew something else they might not. When a large company took over a smaller one, they almost always brought in their own management team. That meant she'd be one of the first ones booted out the door. So much for money and power.

"Obviously, you didn't come here to just dump this information on me," Ashley said.

"You've got a relationship with the old man," Cherry pointed out.

"And the young one, too," Jean added.

"That's debatable," Ashley said.

"No, it's fact," her mother retorted. "I saw the way he looked at you when he came to dinner."

Her mother's imagination must have been working overtime that night. She would admit to an attraction to Max. But that was nothing she couldn't handle. Nor did she want to discuss or debate the issue.

Ashley looked from one woman to the other and said with all the maturity she could muster, "So?"

"Find out what's going on," the two women said together.

"But be subtle," Jean added. "Then we can figure out what, if anything, we can do about it."

"I don't think I'm the best person to approach Max," Ashley protested. "One of you should talk to him."

Jean shook her head. "It's not a good idea to breach the hierarchy. You're in management so it's more logical for you to do it."

Information was about the only power to be had, Ashley realized. If she had to send out résumés, find another job, make a move, now would be the time. It was easier to get a job when you had one. But didn't this just fry her grits. Her family had always been there for her. She wanted to repay them for helping her get through college. She'd been counting on her promotion at CCC to do that.

"All right. I'll see what I can do," she reluctantly agreed. "But I still think someone else should go. This is a bad idea," she muttered.

Because it meant initiating a conversation with Max, a prospect that made her pulse quicken and her heart skip.

Max's intercom buzzed. "Yes, Bernice?"

"Ashley Gallagher to see you, sir."

He had an instant visual of freckles, feminine curves and fiery curls. The image made him smile. "Send her in."

Several moments later, there was a knock on his door just before it opened. "Max?"

He swiveled away from his computer and met her gaze. "Ashley. Come in. What's up?" Besides his pulse rate. "Is this about the memo I sent regarding your specialties budget? Because—"

"No. The changes you made were fine. In fact I think the way you trimmed was smart. I wish I'd seen it myself."

Absurdly, her approval pleased him. "It's nothing more than experience. You're doing a good job."

"Thanks."

When her pleased smile generated a small dimple in her right cheek, he had the most insane desire to trace the soft little indentation. Fortunately, his desk between them kept him from doing anything stupid.

This was business. With an effort, he brought his concentration under control.

"If it's not your budget, then what can I do for you?"

"Something has come to my attention."

He frowned. "I have been getting funny looks from everyone around here lately."

"Has anyone told you you're paranoid?"

"If the shoe fits... And my paranoia makes me wonder if you drew the short straw."

"Excuse me?"

The way her forehead wrinkled in confusion made her look—thoughtful, cute, sexy. And he needed to get out more. Hell, he needed to get out, period.

"Were you chosen to be the bearer of some bad news? Like you're planning another employee gathering for me?"

She cringed. "Not on a bet."

Dressed in a light green silk suit—pencil-thin skirt and jacket that clung to her small waist and curvy hips—she was like a breath of fresh air. Spring. The comparison was even more appropriate because she smelled like a field of flowers. He blinked and let out a long breath. Who hit him with the poetic stick? Since when was he a sweet-talking guy? Since never. Was it being back in Sweet Spring or just being in the presence of this woman that brought out this side of him?

"If it's not business or bad news, to what do I owe this unexpected visit? Are you here to ride me out of town on a rail?"

She laughed. "I don't think I could take you all by myself."

"No?" If she smiled like that again, she could take him easy.

"No." She shifted her feet and looked at the floor for a moment before meeting his gaze. "I'm here to ask you out to dinner."

He couldn't have been more shocked if she'd walked into his office and started a striptease. "Why?"

"Do I need a reason?" she asked, hedging.

Throwing caution to the wind, he stood and walked around his desk, stopping a foot away from her. If he wanted, he was close enough to pull her into his arms. She met his gaze and took several steps back.

"Yeah." He folded his arms over his chest. "I've made no secret of the fact that I wouldn't mind spending time with you. You, on the other hand, have made it clear that you're not interested. So I have to ask—why would you have a change of heart?"

She linked her fingers together. "The truth is that I feel badly about the welcome reception. It was awkward, and I feel responsible."

"You shouldn't. It wasn't your fault."

"I know. But I feel as if we should make it up to you. And I'm here to do that."

"So you did draw the short straw."

"They just said—" She stopped.

"They?" He watched the pulse in her neck flutter wildly and knew she was nervous.

"I mean, *I* decided to hold out a welcoming hand. Start over, so to speak."

"So to speak," he said. He was getting the distinct impression that his first instinct was correct. Someone had put her up to this. And he had a pretty good idea what "this" was all about. "What's really going on, Ashley? Why are you really here?"

She stared him down for several moments, then threw up her hands. "I told them this was a bad idea, but they insisted."

"Who insisted?"

"Some of the employees," she answered vaguely.

Unless he missed his guess, she'd been dispatched on a fact-finding mission. "Did 'they' suggest that the way to a man's heart was through his stomach? Or did you come up with the dinner invitation all by yourself?"

"I knew I was the wrong person. I'm just not good at this sort of thing."

"Define 'this sort of thing.'"

"Wheedling. You know. To use soft words and flattery to get information."

Yeah, he did know. "Ah."

"I have no experience at this. Now if you want to know strategy for acing an exam, or principles of business psychology, I'm your girl. But getting information from a man—" She shook her head. "That's beyond my sphere of expertise."

"You haven't dated much?" he guessed.

"Not much," she muttered. "Not recently."

He'd gotten that message loud and clear when she'd beaten a hasty retreat after he'd told her she was the reason he'd decided to stay. Handling man-woman situations didn't come easily for her.

And just now, he found he liked her more for answering his direct question with a direct response. She'd abandoned the pretense almost immediately. It meant she was honest. Straightforward. Not a game-player. Nine out of ten women he'd known would have brazened it out.

''What information is it you're trying to worm out of me?'' he asked.

''Worm? What happened to wheedle?'' She met his gaze. ''At least let me buy you dinner. It's the least I can do for the information.''

''A bribe?''

''Bribe is such an ugly word.''

''Okay. I accept your invitation to dinner. But I'm guessing this is about work, and I'd rather leave it here. Why don't we put all our cards on the table first?'' he said.

She sighed. ''All right.''

He indicated the leather wing chair in front of the desk. ''Why don't you sit down?''

She nodded. ''Thanks.''

She settled herself, and he heard the whisper of her nylons as she crossed one shapely leg over the other. Like flint on steel, the sound sent sparks skipping through him. Her skirt, a demure length while she stood in front of his desk, hiked up several inches on her thigh. She didn't have to buy him dinner to find out his secrets. All she had to do was sit there looking like sin-in-waiting.

He leaned a hip on the corner of his desk and looked down at her. And yes, he meant the pose to be intimidating. It annoyed him that she was having a lethal effect on his self-control. Time to pull it together. Because he was running the company—for now. And no matter what job he undertook, he always did it well.

''So what do you want to know?'' he asked.

"There's a rumor that Mr. Caine is going to sell the company. Is it true?"

To his profound disappointment, she uncrossed her legs and tugged her skirt down as far as it would go. But she couldn't conceal her slender ankles, shapely calves, and outstanding knees. And as soon as he unstuck his tongue from the roof of his mouth, he would answer her direct question.

He swallowed hard as he rubbed a hand across the back of his neck. "The truth is, at this moment there are no offers on the table for Caine Chocolate."

She let out a long breath. "Everyone will be so relieved."

"Not so fast."

"What?"

Apprehension darkened her eyes. That bothered him and he didn't like that it did. This was business, not personal. And he wanted to keep it that way.

"My grandfather seemed disappointed about the way the reception turned out."

"He talked to you about that?"

"Yeah."

"So you're aware he put me up to it?"

He was now. "Yeah."

"I'm not sure what that has to do with selling the company," she said frowning.

"He has a pipe dream that I'll fit in here at CCC."

"I got that. But he needs to remember that takes time. And you'll only be here temporarily."

He ran his fingers through his hair. "That's just it, Ash."

"What?"

''I'm getting the feeling that he doesn't want to come back to work.''

''But—'' She sat forward. ''If he doesn't come back, what will happen to the company?''

''That's his problem.''

She froze for several moments, then seemed to recover herself. ''Will he appoint someone to take over permanently?''

''Maybe you?''

''I'm not qualified yet. But eventually I'll have the experience to do it justice.''

''I wish that was his vision,'' he said, meaning it sincerely.

''His vision?''

''He told me in no uncertain terms that if there's not a family member at the company controls, he'll sell Caine Chocolate.''

''Does he mean you?''

''I'm the last of the Mohicans,'' he said. ''Or should I say Caines? There's no one else to take over.''

He watched her assimilate the information and found her expression fascinating. It was on the tip of his tongue to say she was beautiful when her thought processes were chugging along at the speed of light. But when her expression turned troubled, he felt something twist in his chest.

''So it's true?'' she asked, tension wrapping around each word. ''He's going to sell the company?''

He nodded. ''Unless I agree to stay.''

Chapter Seven

Ashley put her briefcase on the dining room table Max had just cleared. She'd invited him out to dinner, but somehow he'd turned the tables on her. They'd ended up at the guest house on the Caine family estate. Under normal circumstances, she would have declined his alternative dinner suggestion and told him where he could stick it. But her life hadn't been normal since Max Caine had returned. And she didn't need a conference with her mother and Cherry Addison to tell her what she needed to do next.

After Max had confirmed the rumors, her focus instantly changed from counting the days until his departure to a strategy for convincing him to stay and take over the company permanently. Funny how a worse alternative could make you appreciate the bad you knew.

As she glanced around the guest house, Ashley oohed and aahed to herself. An overstuffed chair and love seat covered in beige plaid were arranged in front of a rock fireplace and gave the area a feeling of intimacy and warmth. The ceiling, comprised of planks, and the wood floor continued the comfortable, country feel. In the dining room, an oak hutch rested against the wall. The matching ball-and-claw foot table was large enough to accommodate six chairs.

As she pulled some files from her briefcase and set them on the table, Max walked in from the kitchen with their refilled wineglasses. He stared at the paperwork. ''So you weren't kidding about a public relations blitz?''

''Not a chance. Were you hoping?''

''Of course.''

''Sorry. There are things you need to know about because they require your approval for the release of funds.'' When she met his gaze, there was an intensity in his eyes she'd never noticed before. ''Is it all right if I put these things on the table?''

She looked at the heavy oak and resisted the urge to run her hand over the beautiful wood. He'd made a phone call to Chip the butler and when they'd arrived, placemats had been laid out with china, silver and crystal for two. A warming tray in the kitchen held a fabulous chicken casserole. Warm bread and a salad had completed the dinner. Her third with Max, but this one by far the most intimate. Meals with only a man and a woman tended to be that way. Part of her was thrilled at the prospect of being alone with him. The other part missed her mother and sister with every fiber of her being.

''Sure,'' he said. ''It won't hurt the wood.''

''I never knew this guest house was here. You can't

see it from the road. And I drove by a lot." She hoped he didn't think she'd been a lovesick moron. Or worse—a stalker. But by the time she'd gotten her driver's license, he'd been gone almost two years. "The estate is on the way to town," she clarified.

"I know." He put her glass beside the stack of files.

She glanced around. "You said there are three bedrooms?"

"And three baths. An exercise room and an office."

"This is bigger than my house."

A frown drew his sandy-colored eyebrows together. "When my parents and I visited, we used to stay here."

"Home away from home," she said.

"Not exactly." His expression was wry. "My mother called it the neutral zone. She and Bentley didn't get along."

"Why is that?" she asked, wondering if he would answer.

"He blamed her for the fact that my father chose not to go into the family business."

"But you came here for visits," she pointed out. "They must have buried the hatchet."

He sipped his wine. "After I was born, Bentley tried to smooth things over. He finally had an heir and didn't want to blow it." He laughed but there was no humor in the sound.

"I'm sure it wasn't all about having an heir," she said. "He loves you."

He shrugged. "This would be a really good time for you to show me the material you've brought."

Ashley had a couple dozen questions she wanted to ask him. How did he feel about all that family turmoil?

About losing his parents? What was it like coming to live with his grandfather? Did he have any connection to the family business even though he'd been away for ten years? But one look at his face told her he'd shut down tighter than lockup at the local penitentiary. For the moment, her public relations blitz was the lesser of two evils. Strike while the iron was hot.

She settled herself near the material she'd arranged then drew in a breath when he pulled out the chair beside her and sat. Speaking of hot, the warmth from his body was unmistakable and distracting. But she was determined to ignore her response.

Opening a file she said, "This is the child care center. It's subsidized by the company. The employees who avail themselves of the services are charged a nominal amount. But the center is open to the general public who pay the full cost. It has a progressive program to stimulate learning, creativity, and social interaction." She met his gaze and struggled to suppress a smile. "You could have used that last one."

"Hmm." One corner of his mouth quirked as he took the glossy brochure.

When their fingers brushed, she could have sworn sparks flew. Or maybe it was just his closeness that made her feel like she could go up in flames. The scent of his aftershave was more intoxicating than her glass of chardonnay. Heat from his body burrowed inside her, warming her everywhere. The brush of his arm against her own started tingles chasing up and down her spine. Apparently his social interaction was functioning just fine.

She picked up another file and noticed that her hand was shaking. Setting the file on the table again, she slid it over to him. ‘‘This is information about the summer activities held at the park. They’re structured for older children and teenagers.’’

He leafed through the data. ‘‘Sports, swimming, cooking classes, art, crafts.’’

‘‘CCC is the primary patron of this program. Without it, kids too old for traditional child care would have a lot of unsupervised time on their hands while their parents are at work.’’

‘‘A worthy endeavor. If self-serving.’’

‘‘Not really,’’ she denied. ‘‘Nowadays most families need two incomes whether child care programs exist or not. But this way, when the kids get too big for a baby-sitter, they don’t run wild.’’

‘‘Like I did?’’

She decided to ignore his comment. ‘‘It’s good for the town as well as the company.’’

‘‘I see.’’

She handed him the last file. ‘‘The Sweet Spring Spartans high school football team went to the championships last year.’’

‘‘What does it say on their jerseys?’’ he asked, squinting at an eight by ten photo of the team.

‘‘No Caine, no gain. I know it’s corny,’’ she said, meeting his wry look. ‘‘But football is big in Texas. And sports build character.’’

‘‘As opposed to adversity,’’ he said pointedly.

‘‘No. I believe I said adversity reveals character.’’

‘‘Ah. My mistake.’’

Hers had been getting this close to him. But if she ran now, she’d look like the coward she was. This attraction for Max scared her. It left her vulnerable whether he stayed or left. She didn’t want to be hurt.

How had she let herself get sucked into the role of recruiter? Especially since face to face was the best way to recruit.

Her task was to show him why he should stay. ''In addition to being one of the team sponsors, CCC funds scholarships for deserving high school seniors.''

His penetrating gaze met her own. ''Didn't you tell me you were working at the company while you went to high school?''

''Yes.''

''And were you deserving of a scholarship?''

''My grades were good,'' she hedged.

''So what are you saying? Did you receive one or not? As the saying goes—charity begins at home.''

''I was offered a four-year scholarship, yes.'' Darn it. What was it about him that made her spill her guts and spell out all the minute details?

''Offered? But you didn't take it? What aren't you telling me, Ash? You had the grades and the determination. Why didn't you use the financial help given by the company?''

''What makes you think I didn't?'' she hedged.

''You told me you worked full time to pay for college.''

She sighed. It hadn't been her finest hour and with all her heart she wanted to bury the incident forever. But she sensed that dodging the question completely wouldn't work with him. Her only alternative was to toss him a crumb without giving him all the ugly details.

''I didn't use the scholarship because it was for a specific school and I didn't want to go there. It meant leaving town. The company gave it to someone else and I enrolled at the local junior college instead.''

He leveled his narrowed gaze on her and seemed to see all her secrets. ''I don't buy it. Everything points to you being an achiever. It doesn't add up that you'd turn your back on the opportunity of a four-year free ride.''

''You're not going to let it drop, are you?'' she asked.

''I'm not planning to, no.''

Apparently it had been too much to hope he wouldn't notice that she'd left out a few details in her story. Her goal in spending this time with him had been to spell out what the community would lose if CCC no longer existed. She couldn't do that while he was fixated on her. If revealing her humiliation would be for the greater good, then so be it.

''All right. Here's the unvarnished truth. I was book smart, not street smart. I fell in love with my high school sweetheart and didn't want to leave him. I decided to stay at home and go to the local junior college. That's why I turned down the financial help.''

''I see.'' He closed the file. ''What happened to Romeo?''

She lifted one shoulder. ''Curse of the Gallagher women strikes again.''

''He left.''

''Six months after I graduated from high school.''

''And you had to work full time, slowing down the higher education process,'' he said.

''That's right. Sadder but wiser,'' she answered.

''So I was right when I said you're smarter than the average bear. Just not about men.''

"Chemistry wasn't one of my best subjects, no," she admitted. If it was, she'd have a better chance of ignoring her physiological responses to Max's male vibes. "But I didn't come here to talk about me. We've gotten way off the subject."

"Have we?"

"Yes." But his smoldering gaze said he wasn't unhappy about the subject. That made her feel like Red Riding Hood to his big bad wolf. "I—I wanted to show you how important Caine Chocolate is to this town and the people in it. There's a symbiotic relationship between the two. Maybe even more than the fact that each benefits the other. I'm not sure one could exist without the other."

In her eagerness to convince him of what she was saying, Ashley half turned and leaned toward him. His already smoky gaze seemed to catch fire as he looked at her mouth. The next thing she knew, he'd threaded his fingers into her loose hair and drew her toward him. Her heart hammered against the wall of her chest. He was going to kiss her. The part of her mind not cheering told her to nip this in the bud. If only she could obey that tiny little voice. But the urgency to know what it felt like to kiss Max Caine couldn't be denied.

Then his mouth settled over hers and rational thought ceased altogether. But her senses kicked in big time. He tasted of wine and sensuality. Instead of being unnerved, the thought thrilled and excited her. His large, strong hand cupped the back of her head to make the touch of their lips firmer. He smelled of cologne and male, a blend more intoxicating than any alcohol she'd consumed. Her arm was resting on the table and he stroked it from wrist to shoulder, leaving a trail of sparks and tingles that burrowed inside.

Liquid heat settled in her center and spread outward. Her breathing quickened into a rhythm that matched his. As he cupped her cheek in his warm palm, he nibbled a path from the corner of her mouth and over her jaw to the hollow beneath her ear. His tongue on that ultrasensitive spot nearly drove her over the edge. The edge of what, she wasn't sure.

Which was why she had to stop this. She pulled back and stared at him as she struggled to draw in air and get her breathing under control. His eyes were like the twin blue flames of a jet's afterburners. Tension rolled from him in nearly tangible waves. Now what?

This was the downside of being dating-challenged. She had no practice in awkward post-kiss conversation. The fact that he was her boss added a dynamic she didn't even want to think about when her mind was fully functional again.

"Say something, Ash." His voice was hoarse and his hand unsteady as he tucked a strand of hair behind her ear.

As she stared at him, all she could think to say was, "Why did you do that?"

"Because I wanted to." His mouth curved up at the corners.

A wave of yearning crashed through her to kiss him again. Was that how he'd felt? "Why did you want to?"

"You were so passionate in making your case about the connection between the company and the town—" He lifted one broad shoulder in a shrug. "Passion is contagious. I got carried away."

Just before making her case, she'd told him about her bump in the romance road. "Was that a pity kiss?" she asked before she could censor herself.

He blew out a long breath. "If anything I feel sorry for the jerk who walked away from a woman like you."

"That's very sweet but not especially comforting coming from you. You're cut from the same cloth. The kind who walks away."

"There are differences. I don't make promises."

"So any woman who gives up something for you, does it with her eyes wide open?"

"I would never let a woman give up something for me."

"So you're a love 'em and leave 'em kind of guy?"

"No. I'm more of a let's have a mutually good time while we can sort of man."

"I see."

He ran his fingers through his hair. "On that note, let's get everything out in the open. This public relations campaign," he put his open palm on the pile of folders she'd just shown him. "This is about convincing me to stay and run the company. Right?"

She drew in a shuddering breath. "Yes."

"I've been clear from the beginning about my intentions. Why would you think I'd change my mind?"

She stood up and backed away from him. While she was this close, all she could think about was how good it had felt to finally kiss him. Her imagination hadn't come close to the sublime reality. But this was a conversation that needed her full attention—or as much of it as she could pull together.

"I think your life is empty." She shook her head. "I don't think it. I know it."

"How?"

"You just told me. You never make promises. You put the brakes on relationships. Though what you do may be too superficial to call it a relationship."

"Is that so?"

"Yes," she said, warming to her subject. "And furthermore, I think you're looking for something of substance in your life."

"Oh?" He folded his arms over his chest. A glint of amusement chased the intensity from his gaze.

"Why else would you finally come back after ten years?"

"Maybe to see my grandfather who'd fallen ill?"

"Exactly. Because he was sick and it might be your last chance. Up until now you've ignored all his overtures. But I believe you were worried about him. You wanted to patch things up with your only family while there was still time."

"Don't romanticize this, Ash. I'm basically a bastard at heart. My grandfather knew it ten years ago and nothing has changed."

"Baloney." She put her hands on her hips. "You've changed. You've grown up but you've been alone. I think there's a part of you that wants more. That doesn't want to be alone and yearns for something permanent. Something you can count on."

"Now who's hoping? But if your theory is correct, then I should be ripe to stay and fit in. If I do, the company won't be sold."

"I'll admit that's the ultimate goal. But I think I'm right about the rest, too."

He shook his head. ''What if you're not? What if I want no part of the family business? No ties? No encumbrances?''

''I'd like an opportunity to change your mind.''

A half smile curved his mouth. ''Oh?''

That hadn't come out right. ''Give Sweet Spring a chance to win you over. This is a great town with salt-of-the-earth people. It's a good place to live. Let me show you that I'm right.''

''I have a consulting contract pending that would start just after Labor Day.''

''Give me until then to show you how good this town can be.''

''You're on.''

When she arrived home, Ashley found her mother and sister waiting for her. The late news was on TV.

Ashley set her purse on the coffee table and sat down on the couch. ''Hi.''

''Where have you been?'' Jean asked, hitting the off button on the TV remote.

''With Max.''

Colleen's slouch disappeared when she sat up and scooted forward. ''With Max where? On a date? Dinner? Movie? Watching the submarine races?''

''His place,'' she answered, sliding a wry look at her sister.

''Did you ask him if the rumors about selling the company are true?'' her mother asked.

Ashley nodded. ''He confirmed that his grandfather is adamant about a family member running it. If Max won't agree to stay, then Mr. Caine is going to put out the word that he'll entertain buyout offers.''

"I was afraid of that," Jean said.

"There's no need to panic just yet." Ashley looked from one to the other.

"I'd just as soon panic now as later," Jean said.

"Mom, I'm surprised at you. He hasn't left yet. And maybe he won't. It's not like you, to go to the bad place without considering a positive strategy."

Her mother tucked her feet up under her. "What strategy would that be?"

"I dazzled him with company public relations programs to show him how closely linked Caine Chocolate is with the community. That's why I was at his place. As soon as he confirmed the rumors, I knew I needed to do something to change his mind about leaving."

"I hope you did more than pull out the eight by ten glossy brochures," Colleen said.

"I did some talking, too," she said vaguely.

Colleen shook her head, obviously disapproving. "This situation calls for action, talking is optional."

"Are you implying I should sleep with him?" Ashley said, shocked.

"Correct me if I'm wrong, sis. And no pun intended, but isn't it true that all of us have a lot riding on him. Including you."

"I can't believe you would say something like that," Ashley huffed. "That's so—"

"Gotcha," her sister said with a grin. "You're way too easy, Ash."

Jean held up her hand. "There will be no sleeping with anyone to convince him of anything."

"Thank you, Mother," Ashley said, shooting her

sister a mom's-on-my-side look. But the memory of the kiss she'd shared with Max warmed her cheeks.

"What did you talk about?" Colleen asked.

"I got him to agree to let me convince him that this is a great place to live and he'd be a fool to pass up the opportunity."

"*Let* you convince him?" Colleen grinned. "You do realize that now he *thinks* you're going to sleep with him?"

"He's wrong. Not even flirting. He's my boss. It would be demeaning and politically incorrect."

"Flirting with the boss," her sister mused.

"Flirting with disaster," Ashley countered. "Considering the family curse, any kind of romantic overture would be the fastest way to *guarantee* he'd leave town. Since he's not the sticking around kind to begin with, we have to come up with a different strategy. And it better be good. Because getting him to agree to run the company is a long shot at best."

"So I'm right to go straight to panic," Jean said.

"Not necessarily. Although it's true he has no love lost for his grandfather and originally only intended a short visit. On the other hand, I don't believe he intended to stay this long."

"If you sleep with him, he might stay longer," Colleen said helpfully.

Both Ashley and their mother glared at her. "That would be sacrificing my integrity. I'm not stupid enough to give up anything for a man who's made no secret of the fact that he's leaving."

Colleen tossed a strand of hair over her shoulder. "It can't hurt to show him what he's missing. Sweet Spring is a wonderful place to live and raise a family."

''Like I said, he's not the staying kind. I don't think Max is interested in a family,'' Ashley said. His name on many most-eligible-bachelor lists supported her theory. ''I'm sort of hoping his Caine genes will kick in and running the company will grow on him. But tonight he mentioned that his father opted out of the family business and the elder Mr. Caine blamed Max's mother for that decision. So the genes might not be any help.''

''I remember something about that. A scandal at the time,'' her mother said, tapping her lip thoughtfully. ''But there's another way to look at it. Max is a different generation. And maybe someone working in the company can convince him it's where he belongs.''

Ashley nodded. ''That's my plan.''

''And it's a good one,'' her mother said. ''Just remember, Ashley. Everyone at CCC is counting on you.''

''But no pressure,'' her sister added with a wicked grin.

Actually, the pressure of resisting Max's assault on her senses was far worse than any burden regarding her co-workers. They were simply resisting change; if she was unsuccessful in convincing Max to stay, many of them would still have jobs in the event of a buyout. But spending time with Max could be detrimental to her heart—whether he stayed or left. So this is what between a rock and a hard place felt like.

A very unsettling place to be.

But she would do her best to help out her CCC family. If that meant flirting with the boss, then so be it.

Chapter Eight

"Nice hit, Max. A game winner. Good thing you were on our side."

"Glad I could help, Scott." Max waved a farewell. It had been a little over a week since his dinner with Ashley at the guest house. And here he was playing on the company softball team.

He watched the younger man headed for the parking lot, a college student home for the summer and working at CCC in distribution. Reminded him of himself. Except he didn't think he'd ever been that young. Max sat on the bleacher seat and took a bottle of Gatorade from his duffel.

"Way to go, hero." Ashley sat next to him. "A home run."

"Hey, Max." Randy Donnelly walked between the bleachers and the chain-link fence that set off the park's baseball field and the red clay with the chalked-off diamond. "This is our lucky day. Glad you came out to join the team."

"Thanks." No point in saying he wasn't a team player. There was no *I* in team and he was an "I" kind of guy.

Ashley cleared her throat loudly and with exaggerated energy as she looked from Randy back to him. "Excuse me. I think I deserve some credit for convincing him to show up."

She deserved all the credit, Max thought.

"Glory hog," Randy scoffed at her. "Anyway, we've got the diamond reserved every Wednesday night after work. Max, we could sure use a bat like yours. And your glove's not bad either."

"I'll keep that in mind," Max said.

Randy nodded and started to turn away. "A bunch of us go to The Fast Lane for something to eat after the game. Why don't you come by?"

"I'll think about it," he said.

"We'll see you there, Randy," Ashley told him. She glanced at Max and shrugged. "Since I'm driving..."

"Okay. Good. See you." Randy slung his sports bag over his shoulder then headed through the trees to the gravel parking lot.

Max didn't delude himself that this after-work baseball game was anything more than blatant brownnosing. The CCC rumor mill had been working overtime. By now everyone was aware that if Max didn't take over, the company would be sold. In that event, some employees would be retained, but no one wanted to take a chance. That's why they wanted him here. He'd agreed because of Ashley. Hanging with her was a very pleasant way to spend his time while he waited for his grandfather to be well enough to reassume control of the company.

"So," she said, "did you have a good time?"

How did he answer that question? He'd liked playing the infield, especially when she'd bumped into him while running the bases. The full body contact, with all the finer parts of hers connecting with the hardest parts of his, worked for him in a big way.

"I had a good time," he said simply.

"So you're not sorry I talked you into coming?"

"No." Max brushed his forearm over his forehead. "Even though I know what's going on."

She licked her index finger and made a "one" in the air. "Score one for you. What's going on?"

"A company conspiracy to get me to change my mind about sticking around."

"Is it working?" she asked, one red-gold eyebrow rising.

"Let's just say it's better than sitting at home watching the Travel Channel."

Ashley took a long drink from her bottle of water. After wiping the moisture from her full bottom lip, she said, "You looked like you were having fun."

Looking at her mouth gave him ideas for fun. Like a repeat of their kiss. She'd asked him why he'd done it and he'd answered that her passion about the bond between the company and the town was contagious. The truth was he'd wanted to channel that passion in a different direction, a personal direction. Instead of taking the pressure off his feelings, that fleeting meeting of mouths only whetted his appetite for more. But now that he had her attention, he had serious reservations. He didn't want to be part of the Gallagher curse.

She shifted under his intense scrutiny. Actually, it was more of a squirm. "You're a pretty good baseball player."

He capped his Gatorade. "I'm athletic. But you know as well as I do they would have accepted me on the team even if I couldn't do more than stand in for third base."

"They genuinely liked you, Max. And they're trying to bond. Give them another chance to welcome you to the CCC team."

He met her brown-eyed gaze and sighed. There'd been a time when he might have enjoyed being a part of all this. But now...

"There's not much point in my bonding with them," he said. "We both know that."

She tilted her head slightly as she studied him. "You have a reputation as a 'fixer,' someone who does what needs to be done to save a company. That includes saving companies as well as dismantling them."

"That's true."

"But it's always short term."

"Right again," he said. "When the job is done, I go on to the next one."

"Don't you ever have the urge to stick around and see the fruits of your labor?"

"No." Although lately he'd noticed a general dissatisfaction in his life. An underlying restlessness.

"You've never had the urge to stay and watch the results of something you've put into motion?"

"Not really. I like the short-term victory. Nothing

lasts,'' he said, thinking about the loss of his parents. He'd thought of them a lot since telling Ashley about his father's defection from the family company. ''Nothing is forever.''

''So you don't even try? You just give up and turn your back?''

He looked at her. ''Well if it isn't little Miss-do-as-I-say-not-as-I-do.''

''What are you talking about?''

''Curse of the Gallagher women. You're hiding. You don't try. You've turned your back.''

''And you know this—how?''

He met her gaze directly. ''I have the scars from your numerous rejections to prove it. You turned down all invitations of a social nature until my grandfather confirmed his intention to sell the company if I leave. And your turn-downs were motivated by your emotional baggage and that of your family.''

''Even if you're right, and confirmation of that will never pass my lips, what's it to you? Why do you want to have a drink with me?''

''Has it occurred to you that you've damaged my pride? Deflated my ego?''

''No.'' Her eyes widened. ''And I could come up with a dozen zingers. Like it would take more than a rejection from me to deflate an ego the size of Texas. But I'll refrain.''

''Taking the high road. Good for you.'' One corner of his mouth quirked up.

''Why would you want to spend time with me?''

''Call it a healthy dose of curiosity.''

''About?''

"You. What do you want, Ashley? What's important to you?"

"Lots of things."

"Okay. I'll narrow it down. What do you want out of life? A career?"

"Money and power," she murmured.

"What?" he leaned closer, catching the floral scent of her skin. The fragrance was like a flash-and-bang grenade bursting inside him, generating a heat blast that had nothing to do with the humidity. And everything to do with her.

"Nothing." As if in a daze, she shook her head. "What do I want? For one thing, I'd like to make sure my mother and sister never again have to worry about where the mortgage money is coming from."

"Times were tough?"

She nodded. "Especially while I was going to school. But they never once suggested I do anything except get my college degree. Without their unwavering support, I don't think I could have done it."

"Okay. But beyond taking care of them, what do you want for yourself?"

"Job security." She slid him a look that said he was single-handedly responsible for that.

"And?" He met her gaze.

The freckles dusting her nose made him want to trace it with his finger. Her red curls were in wild disarray around her small face, as if a man had run his hands through the strands while making love to her. The thought kicked his breathing up to the unsteady range in zero point three seconds. In less time than that, he could be tasting her lips.

"And what?" she said.

He huffed out a breath. ''Don't you want a family of your own? Husband? Kids?''

''I haven't had time to think about it,'' she hedged. ''My focus has been on getting my degree. Then my promotion. I want to build a career.''

''Money and power,'' he said, repeating her words.

''Yes,'' she answered, an odd expression on her face.

''What is it?''

''It's too silly.''

''Try me.''

She tucked her hair behind her ear. ''Promise me you won't call the men in the white coats.''

''Okay.''

''I was born on February twenty-ninth.''

''So you told me. A leap year baby.''

''Yes. My two best friends, Rachel Manning and Jordan Bishop were born the same day, same hospital, twenty-four years ago.''

He did the math. ''That means you actually had a birthday this year.''

''We celebrated in New Orleans,'' she said nodding. ''I took a long weekend.''

''That's right. You mentioned it before. Good for you. All work and no play—'' Somehow he didn't think anything could make Ashley a dull girl.

''Anyway, to make a long story short, we did a good deed and returned a tacky brass lamp that had been stolen from a shop in the French Quarter. The Gypsy owner told us to rub the lamp and make a wish.''

''Did you?''

''We played along.'' She nodded. ''Rachel wished

for a baby. Jordan wanted to be a princess and live in a palace.''

He grinned. ''Don't tell me. You asked for money and power.''

''Yes.''

''So, did your wish came true?''

She lifted one shoulder. ''Your grandfather says he got the idea for my promotion while I was in New Orleans. That's suspicious enough. But the other thing that makes me wonder is that Rachel now has a baby. She's the permanent guardian for an infant left in her care.''

''Coincidence,'' he said automatically.

''Probably,'' she admitted. ''At any rate, my focus has been my family, my education and now my career. And that means my CCC family. And it *is* extended family.''

He wouldn't know about that. He'd lost his own. He'd had nowhere to go but to his grandfather. For six years they'd endured an uneasy truce, then the old man showed how he really felt. What would it have been like to feel a part of the company? To never question his acceptance? If his parents had lived… No point in going there.

But when he looked at Ashley, at the intensity that leapt into her eyes, he knew she meant what she said. She was committed to CCC on several levels. What would it be like to have her passionate, unquestioning loyalty? He shook his head. That kind of thinking was dangerous. Next, he'd be thinking about sticking around. But permanence was something he never wanted to do.

"CCC is a family working overtime to include me in the ranks," he said.

"Whatever. Like you said—beats Travel Channel reruns." She stood. "Let's go get something to eat."

His gaze lifted from her slender legs, past her curvy hips and trim waist, over her firm breasts to her full lips, sparkling eyes, and flaming red curls. She was definitely full of flash. It was the bang part that gave him pause. So it was a good thing she was focused on career and company, to the exclusion of everything else. Because if he wasn't careful, she could take him down.

"You're on. I'll buy," he said.

He'd bought more than a few times in the last month, Ashley thought, as she and Max walked out of the Sweet Spring Cinema. The high humidity of a Texas night in August hit them hard after the air-conditioned theater. She realized he'd been running the company for about eight weeks now. For the last four, he'd played baseball every Wednesday after work. And he'd asked her out regularly, tonight being no exception. Although he hadn't kissed her again. The brotherly good-night kiss on the cheek at her door didn't count. And since when was she counting?

Since now. And that made her think about what he'd said to her at the park, the first time he'd played ball. He was curious about her. What did that mean? But more importantly, why did she care? And how could she stop thinking about it? This was making her crazy. He was making her crazy.

"What did you think of the movie?" he asked, looking down at her.

"Weird." She glanced around at the other people leaving the theater. "You know, Max, I've been thinking about a new specialty item for—"

He put a finger over her lips to silence her. "No work talk."

Her eyes widened. "I don't understand."

"You're a bright girl. What part of let's talk about something besides Caine Chocolate don't you get?" He stuck his hands in the pockets of his shorts.

"We both know what this is about."

"It's about the opportunity to give Sweet Spring a chance to win me over."

"That's right. The town and the company are intertwined," she pointed out not for the first time. "So this is not a date. Shop talk shouldn't be off limits."

"Technically. But for tonight, let's not talk about work. Let's just be a man and a woman out on a—"

"Don't you dare say date." She stopped and turned on him.

He looked surprised. "Okay. What do you suggest we call it?"

"How about we're just a man and woman out for a movie and dinner."

"Friends," he said, a note of amusement in his voice.

Were they? Had they picked up where they'd left off ten years ago? Hanging out with Max was not her first choice. It was her only choice. She had to play this his way as long as there was still time to convince him to stay. But friends? She'd be lying if she said she didn't like him.

"Friends works," she agreed. And speaking of

time, she wondered how much more she had. ''How's your grandfather feeling?''

''He seems good.''

''Any word on when he'll be able to come back to work?''

Max shook his head. ''I asked him that a couple days ago.''

Because he was antsy to leave? The thought gave her a hollow feeling smack dab in the center of her chest. ''What did he say?''

''He was vague. Said he feels pretty good, but still tires easily.''

''What does his doctor say?''

''I don't know. I tried getting information out of him, but there's some pesky privacy of information thing. Without permission from Bentley, he couldn't discuss anything with me.''

''So why did you call the doc? Are you ready to be gone?''

The hollow feeling hit her again, a little lower. If this kept up, she'd be empty inside. She wished she could delegate someone else to convince him to stay.

''I hadn't actually thought about it,'' he admitted.

''Can I take that to mean you're having such a good time here you don't want to leave?''

The corners of his mouth tilted up in a sexy grin. ''It only means I've been busy. And speaking of that, what do you want to do now?''

''Your proposal was for a movie and dinner,'' she reminded him.

''Is that little drive-in hamburger place on Walnut Creek still there?''

"Beef 'n' Buns?" She nodded. "Yeah. I haven't been there in ages."

"Me, either. Let's go."

"Works for me."

As they walked down the street to where the car was parked, Ashley noticed a family—mother, father, and two little ones—sitting outside at a café. The little girl was in a high chair and the boy, a bit older, used a booster seat. The children were seriously focused on eating ice cream while the couple talked and laughed.

Ashley felt an ache deep inside, an emptiness that she'd never noticed before. She glanced over her shoulder. There was nothing especially noteworthy about the young family, which made her reaction even more strange. She tripped where a crack in the sidewalk lifted the concrete.

Max took her arm to steady her. "You okay?"

"Yeah." She slid her purse strap more securely on her shoulder.

"Here's the car." He hit the keyless entry then opened the door for her.

After handing her inside, he got in and they drove to the burger place. Max placed their orders through the speaker, then they sat in silence for several minutes.

"Something bothering you, Ash?"

She glanced over at him in the driver's seat. "Why do you ask?"

"First of all, you're uncharacteristically quiet."

That statement implied that he'd catalogued her characteristics. "What's second?"

"You answered a question with a question. Classic stall tactic."

It was on the tip of her tongue to ask why he would think she was stalling, but his comment sank in. "You made the rule no talking about business. Maybe I've got nothing to say."

"A scrappy lady like you is never at a loss for words. So what's bothering you?"

He was dead on. How had he learned to read her so well? And when did he get bit by the sensitivity bug? But she remembered all those lunches with him during that summer ten years ago. He was the one who'd sat with her. Maybe he'd always been sensitive. It was possible his cool, carefree, controlled exterior was the hard shell protecting his soft gooey center. Now *there* was a characteristic.

What did she have to lose by telling him the truth? "It's your fault, actually."

"Mine?" He looked at her, a surprised expression on his face.

"Ever since you asked me what I want out of life, I've been thinking about the question."

"What's the answer?"

"I do want a family, children."

"What about a husband?"

"I wouldn't have children without one." But that meant letting down her guard and taking a chance on a man. She wasn't sure she could do that.

Just then the Beef 'n' Buns babe brought a tray laden with burgers, fries and sodas. She hooked it onto the side of the car and Max paid her.

"Keep the change," he said.

The pretty brunette stared at the money in her hand. When she did the math, her eyes lit up. "Thanks a lot."

"Don't mention it."

Max handed over her food and Ashley piled napkins in her lap. She unfolded her cheeseburger and took a bite. "It's pretty much understood that a woman would want a husband to go along with children. I think your question implies that you're stereotyping me because of my upbringing."

"No." He chewed on a french fry. "Maybe," he admitted.

"It's because of the way I grew up that I don't want to raise children without a father."

"But you're devoted to your mother and sister."

"True. But that doesn't mean I didn't miss having a dad. When I was a kid, I used to watch families and get this weird sort of aching empty feeling inside. Rachel and I used to hang out at Jordan's because she was the only one of us who had even the semblance of a normal family."

"I take it her family had their problems?"

"Yeah. Although, as a kid, I couldn't see that." She took a sip of her soda. "But how I envied her for having a father. I desperately wanted a male authority figure in my life to grill my dates. To teach me how to change a tire. To warn me about guys—"

"Like me?"

She grinned. "If the wingtips fit..."

His smile faded as he looked at her. "Do you really think you'd have listened? Teenagers are notoriously defiant and insubordinate."

"Is that the voice of experience talking?"

"Yes," he said. "Teens are rebels, and I was their king."

"Maybe I wouldn't have listened. The point is that

I'll never know. But my life might have been different. If I ever have children, I'd like to have the whole enchilada—mom, dad, little house with a yard and the white picket fence around it. I'm a cliché-in-waiting."

"We're a pair," he said. "I had too much authority and you wanted more. As a rule a man's a fool. When it's hot he wants it cool. When it's cool he wants it hot. Always wanting what is not."

"A poet," she said.

"I can't take credit."

"Where'd you hear it?"

"My grandfather." He shook his head. "I told him once that I wished he'd died instead of my parents."

She sucked in a breath. "Oh, Max—"

"I'd just come to live with him. He caught me sneaking out to do something he'd forbidden me to do."

"And he made up a rhyme?" she asked.

"Yeah." A pensive smile turned up the corners of his mouth. "Then he said if I didn't stay put, he'd hire a bodyguard to see that I did. And he had the capital to back up the threat."

"Did you stay put?"

"Yes." He slid a glance to her. "Funny—I haven't thought about that for a long time."

"But that must have hurt him—what you said."

"I suppose. But then I just thought he was an interfering old man. Now—"

"What?"

"I'm glad he did it."

Ashley had no idea there'd been so much conflict between Max and his grandfather. The situation couldn't have been easy for either of them.

"So he was a male authority figure for you."

"It's safe to say that."

She glanced at him. "So Mr. C. actually domesticated Sweet Spring's resident bad boy."

A frown drew his eyebrows together as he reached over and took her hand in his large, warm one. "I hope you get everything you want, Ash."

Another avoidance tactic. But she didn't mind. Max had given her a glimpse of the wounded, confused teen he'd been and it shook her up. It was easier to think of him as a coldhearted corporate consultant who worshipped the bottom line. She didn't want to feel anything for him, especially sympathy. Which was exactly why she'd wanted to keep her distance from him.

Now she was afraid he would stay. And afraid of what would happen if he didn't.

Chapter Nine

"Here's to health." Bentley Caine held up his red wine.

"To health," Ashley agreed. She had come to the estate for dinner a short while before.

Max thought she looked radiant, with her shiny red curls framing her small face and her sleeveless yellow sundress. It struck him how intensely he'd been anticipating her arrival. Then there was that vague sensation of restlessness he experienced when she wasn't with him. The sight of her full lips always raised his pulse rate and tonight was no exception. He wanted to kiss off the layer of shiny, orangey lipstick that looked freshly applied. Glancing at his grandfather, he checked that feeling. Later, he thought.

"To health," Max said.

His grandfather appeared to have an abundance. Since Max had been there, he'd taken off a few pounds. The gray look in his face was gone, replaced by a robust color. His silver hair was neatly trimmed and in his beige slacks and golf shirt, he was every bit the relaxed lord of the manor. A curious sense of relief trickled through Max.

The three of them were having drinks in the living room while the cook put the finishing touches on dinner. Before tonight, his grandfather had mentioned several times that he should feel free to ask friends over. The old man's suggestions had become less veiled and more specific when he'd mentioned Ashley by name. Until now, Max had resisted, figuring the silver fox had something up his sleeve. Max wasn't sure why his own attitude had shifted enough to ask her over, but he was glad Ash was here.

"Speaking of health," Ashley said. "Is it all right for you to be drinking alcohol, Mr. C.?"

"The latest word from the medical establishment is that a daily glass of red wine lowers the risk of heart attack. And I plan to pursue the practice at every opportunity, before they change their minds."

"Yes, sir," Ashley said. "I know what you mean. Tomorrow they'll say there's a study linking red wine consumption to global warming."

Max watched his grandfather chuckle. The two of them continued their easy interaction, and he felt a tightening in his chest that could be jealousy. He was sure the old man wasn't hitting on her, which meant Max envied their warm camaraderie. If he was stupid enough to confess this to her, Ashley would say he clearly didn't play well with others and he needed to learn to share. Or he needed to go a few rounds with a psychotherapist.

Bentley laughed and shook his head at something

Ashley had said. ''I've missed seeing you, my dear. In fact, I've mentioned to my grandson more than once that he should invite you to dinner.''

Max noticed the gleam in the old man's eyes. ''And here she is,'' he said.

''Like a breath of fresh air,'' his grandfather commented.

''Thank you, Mr. C. So, when are you coming back to work?''

The old man groaned like a creaky gate as he sat on the couch. Max knew for a fact that Bentley Caine moved easily, like a man fifteen years younger. The sound effects were much ado about something.

''Sit, my dear.'' Bentley patted the sofa beside him and Ashley sat. ''I'm anxious to go back to the company. I've inconvenienced my grandson quite enough.'' He shrugged. ''But you know doctors.''

''Caution is good, sir. But we miss you.''

''From all the reports I hear, my grandson is doing a good job,'' he said, glancing at Max.

''Are you keeping tabs on me?''

''He's doing a great job,'' Ashley said, glancing in his direction. ''Everyone is talking about how smoothly the company is running with him at the helm.''

''Of course I'm not keeping tabs on you,'' the old man said as if she hadn't spoken. ''I have many friends at the company. Some of them I've known for twenty-five or thirty years.''

Max sipped his drink. ''I see.''

''One of the things I like most about my job is the continuity of the workforce.'' Ashley's bright, perky tone was at complete odds with the glare she shot him. "There's not a large turnover. It's cost effective."

Bentley nodded. "When I talk to my friends, and it happens frequently, the conversation inevitably turns to business. It's only natural."

"It's true, Max. People talk about the things they have in common," Ashley said. "And CCC is like one big happy family."

"Sure it is," Max snapped. "Another thing that's natural is old habits. They die hard."

Bentley's silver brows drew together in a frown. "Max, don't be vague. Say what you mean."

"You didn't trust me ten years ago. If you're checking up on me, you obviously still don't."

"I made a mistake ten years ago. I jumped to the wrong conclusion. I'm old, not stupid. I'm capable of learning and not repeating blunders. But this reaction of yours makes me wonder if you can say the same."

"Someone recently told me the fruit doesn't fall far from the tree," he said, watching Ashley's cheeks flush with color. "I may have assumed the worst, but you did it first."

"Stop it. Both of you." Ashley set her wineglass on the coffee table and stood.

Was she leaving, Max wondered. The thought chafed and he started toward her. "Now, Ashley—"

"Don't you 'now Ashley' me. You did this the last time I saw you together, the first time you'd been in the same room in ten years. Is it me? Do you start bickering when I'm around?"

"You're being ridiculous," Max said.

"Am I? You two have been living on this estate together since Max came home, but you might as well be on opposite sides of the country. You live in the guest house and he lives here. You keep your distance. And you've settled nothing. All the problems that existed between you ten years ago are alive and well. Don't you people talk to each other? You're family, for Pete's sake.''

''That's not true,'' Bentley said.

''It is true. Your son was Max's father. Consequently you're family.''

''That's not what I meant. The problems that existed between us. They've changed.''

''I stand corrected. How silly of me. Of course they've changed. Distance and noncommunication have created a whole slew of new ones,'' she said.

Bentley shifted uncomfortably. ''I can tell you one thing that's resolved. My grandson is more mature.''

''Can you say the same?'' she shot back.

Max knew it was wrong to be turned on because she was mad, but he couldn't help it. There was her passion again. She was ticked off at both of the Caine men. For once, he and his grandfather were in the same boat.

Bentley frowned at her. ''I don't understand the question.''

''Are you being a grown-up? Have you told Max you're sorry for misjudging him? Did you apologize for not giving him the benefit of the doubt?''

''Well, I—''

''That's what I thought,'' she snapped.

Max smiled. ''Well, that's different. I don't think I've ever spent time in this house with someone on my side.''

She glared at him. "I've got a bone to pick with you, too, buster."

"What does that mean?"

"Have you made any effort to talk to your grandfather? Take the high road and make the first move? Put your grievances on the table? Cleared the air?"

"Well, I—"

"That's what I thought." She shook her head. "I don't think either one of you has matured. You're like two little boys who need a time-out."

"See here, young woman—"

"No, you see here," she said, pointing at his grandfather. "You already had a ten-year time-out. Care to try for twenty? How about the rest of your life? Didn't this health scare teach you anything? Speak up now or you may never get another opportunity."

Max worked hard to suppress a smile. When his grandfather slid a glance in his direction, it was clear he was having the same problem.

"I don't know what to say," Bentley admitted.

Max was a little surprised he didn't seem upset. But then his grandfather had always admired spunk and spirit. Ashley had it in spades. Anyone—man or woman—who would take on two stubborn Caines, was pretty impressive. Scrappy. He'd thought so when he'd come back to town. He hadn't changed his mind. If they had been alone, he would have kissed the living daylights out of her.

"I can't believe this," Ashley sniffed. "It's nothing more than basic courtesy. Do unto others. Mr. Caine, you need to say you're sorry to Max for what you did."

The old man let out a long breath and stood up.

"You're right, my dear. It's too little and ten years too late, but—" He met Max's gaze. "I'm sorry, son."

Max didn't know what to say. But when Ashley turned her indignant glare on him, he figured he'd better come up with a script pretty darn fast.

"Well?" she said to him. "It's your turn."

"What do I have to be sorry for?"

"You took off without trying to talk things through. If you hadn't, all of this could have been avoided. Not only that, for a decade you ignored his attempts at reconciliation. You rebuffed the olive branch he held out. No wonder so many people think of you as the ingrate. You're stubborn and self-righteous. It took a health crisis to get you here. You are each other's only family and your behavior is just plain wrong. Refusing an apology is a special kind of rude. You need to accept your grandfather's apology and say you're sorry to him."

Max blew out a long breath as he looked at the old man. Slowly, he held out his hand. "I'm sorry, Grandfather."

Ashley looked at them and shook her head. "I can't believe I have to teach you everything." She rolled her eyes. "Hallmark moment. Front and center. Hugs, on the double."

Max was sure he saw his grandfather grin. Then he held out his arms and Max slowly rounded the coffee table to give him a quick embrace. The stiff awkwardness went both ways, yet it was oddly liberating. His heart felt lighter somehow.

Max stood beside his grandfather, and they both

looked down at Ashley. "She's pretty formidable. At the company they call her Xena."

"What?" Bentley asked.

"The warrior princess," Max explained.

"Ah. Appropriate."

"They do not call me that," she scoffed. "You're making it up."

"No. I'm making up with my family," he said, and grinned at his father's father.

Thanks to her he could do that.

Then she looked uncertain. "You know, now that the adrenaline rush is winding down, it occurs to me that either or both of you could fire me for insubordination."

Bentley stepped forward. "Fire you? I think you just saved Max a small fortune in analysis costs."

"Me?" he said. "What about you?"

"At my age, I can't remember my inner child and psychoanalysis would be a waste of time and money. Clearly I'm just in my old, eccentric phase."

Max laughed. "And this phase is different from the others—how?"

"Careful, son, we've just cleared the air. Let's not muck up our reconciliation with another quarrel." Bentley grinned.

"Okay." Max returned the grin. "But there's still the question of whether or not to fire our specialty and seasonal manager."

The older man studied her. "Ashley's true specialty is good manners and common sense. Not to mention courage above and beyond the call of duty. Anyone who would take on two Caine men at the same time is deserving of our respect and admiration, not censure."

Max had thought the same thing a few moments ago. Who knew they could ever agree on something? He looked at the old man and an unfamiliar sensation of affection seeped through him. As well as sadness for the years they'd lost. Maybe time truly was the great healer.

"So I'm not fired?" Ashley asked, looking only marginally concerned.

Max and his grandfather exchanged a glance. "No," they said together.

Bentley looked at his watch. "But I'm going to fire cook if dinner isn't ready."

"Cook's been with you for fifteen years. I'm sure she's appropriately intimidated," Max said.

"I'm going to check on things in the kitchen. If you'll excuse me." Without waiting for an answer, he left the room.

Max looked at Ashley. She was too far away. After closing the distance between them, he cupped her face in his hands and tunneled his fingers into the bright, wild silk of her hair.

"I've been wanting to do this ever since you said 'don't you now Ashley me.'"

Her eyes widened as he lowered his head, but she rested her hands on his chest, right over his hammering heart. Then he touched his lips to hers and sighed at their exquisite softness. He traced the seam of her mouth with his tongue and she instantly opened, admitting him inside.

His pulse stuttered and jumped as he imitated the intimate act of making love to her. She tasted of strawberry-flavored lip gloss and wine, and smelled like a meadow in springtime. He breathed in the scent of her and peaceful contentment settled over him at the same time his blood raced through his veins to points south. A contradiction, but true nonetheless. Ashley had that effect on him.

From the time he'd learned his parents were gone forever, he'd felt as if he didn't belong anywhere. But tonight had changed everything. Holding her in his arms made him feel as if he'd come home.

Lifting his head, he felt a shaft of satisfaction noting that her breathing was just as rapid and uneven as his. He sucked in a deep breath. "I bet when you came to dinner you had no idea you'd be the rose between two thorns."

Her lips, still moist from his kiss, curved up in a sweet smile. "Always happy to help."

This was unfamiliar territory, Max realized. He'd wanted women before. And he had no trouble getting what he wanted. But the rules had always been understood: no long-term emotional entanglements. He'd thought Ashley was that kind of woman. Not even close, he'd learned. She was a white picket fence, white lace and vows kind of woman.

And still he wanted her.

"We'd better go see if Grandfather is firing the cook," he said.

"Okay."

He needed to do something to take the edge off his focus and need for her. The last thing he wanted was to hurt her. Tonight he'd discovered that he could go home again.

He just didn't know if he wanted to stay there forever.

* * *

Ashley sat with her friends Rachel Manning and Jordan Bishop in The Fast Lane. Their busy schedules made coordinating a date to get together an uphill battle. But they'd finally managed because it was important to them to touch base once a month. To catch up on each other's news. And after kissing Max a week ago, boy did she have news.

After their salads were delivered, the conversation picked up right where they'd left off.

"So, Rachel, what's going on with you and Jake?" Dark-haired, dark-eyed Jordan speared a piece of avocado with her fork with the same gusto and adventurous spirit that was her approach to life.

Rachel was a Meg Ryan look-alike. Except for her brown eyes. Tonight they glowed with a contentment and happiness Ashley had never seen before.

"Jake and I are getting married. And we have a baby. We're adopting Emma so she'll be ours legally."

"This is his brother's baby? The one the kid left with you before he took off with the baby's mother to play house?" Jordan asked.

"It's not quite as flaky as it sounds," Rachel said. "They wanted to see if they could make a go of it and realized that they were too young for the responsibility of a family. They found out how important an education is. But they both loved their daughter enough to give her to Jake and me. The two of us fell in love with Emma first, then each other," she said dreamily.

Jordan waved her fork in the air. "You do realize your wish came true, don't you?"

"Yeah." Rachel let out a long sigh. "Weird, huh?"

"Coincidence." Ashley wiped her mouth with the white paper napkin. She remembered Max saying the same thing.

"I agree," Jordan said. "After all, I wished to be a princess and live in a palace. At the very least, I'd have to hook up with a prince. And I have to tell you they're pretty scarce on the streets of Sweet Spring, Texas." She looked from Ashley to Rachel. "Do you think wishes have an expiration date?"

"You mean like a shelf life?" Ashley asked with a grin.

"Maybe." Jordan frowned. "If I could do it over, I'd wish for a father who stayed out of my life."

Rachel stared at Jordan as if she had two heads. "Since I've known you, and we go all the way back to the newborn nursery, you've been moaning because your father never spent time with you."

"Rachel's right." Ashley looked at her two friends. "Since when do you want your father to mind his own business?"

"Since our birthday." Jordan sipped from her water glass, then wiped the condensation from her fingers onto her napkin. "Remember that was when he had that mild heart attack—February twenty-ninth."

"Yeah. What does that have to do with butting in?" Ashley asked.

"Ever since, he's been obsessed with putting everything in his life in order—including me."

"How's that?" Ashley asked.

She realized she'd been so preoccupied with her

work and Max, that she hadn't kept up with her friend like she should. She'd baby-sat for Emma. Seeing Rachel and Jake together had given her a clue about the two of them. But all of this about Jordan was breaking news.

Jordan sighed. ''You both know he's a workaholic who built his mega-buck oil business with his own two hands. And I'm his only child. He says that makes me an heiress.''

Ashley took a sip of her iced tea. ''So?''

''Since I went into interior design instead of following in his footsteps, he feels compelled to see that there's a man in my life capable of handling the company after he's gone.''

''He's setting you up with men?'' Rachel guessed.

Jordan nodded. ''The last incident was the worst. He invited me out to the lake house. I was cautiously optimistic that he and I were finally connecting. For the first time in my life, I thought he wanted to spend time with me, to get to know me.''

''Yeah. What happened?'' Ashley asked.

''He didn't show.''

Rachel shrugged. ''That's pretty typical. Disappointing considering your expectation, but 'worst'? I don't get it.''

''He'd arranged for a man to be there. Someone he wanted me to meet.''

''He left you with a complete stranger?'' Ashley was appalled. Abominable behavior even by Harman Bishop standards.

Jordan nodded. ''He's been on a tear ever since I broke it off with Clark Caldwell. He thought the guy had wings, a halo and walked on water. I think he's a self-centered, egotistical, power-hungry jerk. But enough about my problems.'' She looked at Ashley. ''Speaking of power, what's up with you?''

''Certainly not that,'' she said wryly. ''My promotion came with a raise. But I've earned every penny of it. Who knew making a wish come true was such hard work?''

''Is it that? Or the fact that Max Caine is back in town?'' Rachel stuffed a cherry tomato in her mouth.

Just hearing his name made Ashley hot all over.

It must have shown in her face, because Jordan pointed her fork and said, ''You're blushing. I think you're busted, Ash.''

''He's hard work,'' she admitted.

''If I remember correctly, you had a crush on him once upon a time.'' Jordan tucked a strand of her long dark hair behind her ear.

''That was ten years ago and I was only fourteen.''

''Hmm. Defensive. All I said was you *had*—past tense—a crush on him.'' Jordan met her gaze. ''But maybe it's present tense now.''

''I'm still attracted to him.'' Ashley suddenly lost her appetite and pushed her half-eaten salad away.

''So what's the problem?'' Jordan said. ''Are there company rules against flirting with the boss?''

''No. But—''

Ashley thought about the night Max and his grandfather had crossed a big hurdle, apologizing to each other. At her insistence. Since then, something about Max was different, more mellow. She got the feeling he was settling in to the company. Her heart couldn't handle that kind of dangerous wishful thinking.

''But what?'' her friends said together.

Ashley met their questioning gazes. ''Max has his own very successful corporate consulting business. He takes sick companies and either makes them better or dismantles them. So he goes where he's needed.''

''Like Robin Hood.'' Rachel looked at their grins and said, ''What?''

''He's not that romantic,'' Ashley explained. ''He doesn't steal from the rich and give to the poor. He gets paid the big bucks for his expertise. But he's agreed to stay in town to run the company while his grandfather recuperates from his heart attack or until his next consulting contract.''

And the elder Mr. Caine was looking healthy and rested, Ashley realized. Max wouldn't be there much longer. That hollow feeling in her chest yawned wider. It was getting more difficult to shut down her feelings. She was afraid very soon she wouldn't be able to stop them at all. ''Under the circumstances, it wouldn't be very smart to let myself want more than attraction.''

''Sweet Spring scuttlebutt has it that he might stay permanently,'' Jordan said.

Ashley shook her head. ''Nothing more than wishful thinking.''

Rachel looked thoughtful. ''I've heard that wishful thinking is a projection of your heart's desire.''

Jordan grinned. ''What is it about being in love that makes people who are want to take the rest of us down with them?''

''I'm just so happy.'' Rachel sighed. ''And I want my two best friends to feel the same way.''

Ashley plastered a smile on her face because if she didn't she would cry. She envied Rachel, but she was afraid to experience the feeling with Max. And she realized she didn't want to feel it with anyone else. She refused to hope that he'd miraculously have a change of heart about taking over his family's company. Although it was a minor triumph that he and his grandfather had patched things up, that was the extent of the miraculous. And she wouldn't believe otherwise. Because if she did, the next step could be giving up her heart. She'd vowed never again to give up anything for a man.

And giving it to Max would be stupid. She already knew how much it hurt when he went away.

Chapter Ten

"I can't believe it's Labor Day already," Ashley said. She was barbecuing hamburgers and hot dogs. Sitting at the permanent wooden park table beside the grill, her mother was munching on potato chips.

"Time flies when you're having fun," Jean replied.

CCC was celebrating the holiday with its annual company picnic, an event the employees looked forward to every year. Privately, they all wondered if this was the last. Publicly, Ashley had only heard positive feedback that Max hadn't messed with the tradition. In fact, like the rest of administration, he'd volunteered to help with activities. Did that mean anything? Was it a sign?

Ashley fanned the smoke from the grill away from her face, then lined up her barbecue fork, tongs and spatula. The table beside her mother was arrayed with paper plates and napkins, plastic utensils, and condiments. Salads and individual bags of chips were lined up next. Several large tin tubs overflowed with ice and canned sodas. She was in charge of barbecue central.

Her mother took a bite of her hot dog and chewed thoughtfully. ''Next thing you know it will be Christmas.''

Hard to believe on such a warm day. The park tables were shaded by an abundance of trees and a steady breeze made the air comfortable. But in a couple months it would be cold and damp and they'd be getting ready for the holidays.

Ashley blew a strand of hair off her forehead. ''The Halloween product will be going out soon. I'm finalizing a line of items for Valentine's Day.''

Would she have a valentine?

The question made her think of Max. Although she didn't need an excuse. He hovered at the edge of her consciousness pretty much all the time.

She glanced at the activities going on around her. For the last couple of weeks there had been sign-up sheets at the company for various games and activities. In addition to all the food, CCC had provided awards for children's games and drawings for the adults that included DVD players, gift certificates, and the grand prize of a TV. Sack races, the ever popular raw egg carry, three-legged race and the water balloon toss were coming up after lunch. A baseball game was in progress concurrently with the volleyball tournament. Administrative personnel were running the show, their way of showing appreciation for the rank and file employees.

She finally spotted Max with a group of children organizing a tug-of-war. How appropriate, she thought, when she felt a tug on her heart at the sight of him. She'd never thought much about whether or not men had good legs, but looking at Max gave her a completely different point of view, as well as something to appreciate.

He was wearing navy shorts, which showed off well-defined calf muscles and athletic thighs. His shirt had a collar and tab front and the powder blue knit molded to his wide shoulders, the contours of his broad chest and firm abdomen. The shade of the shirt accented his sandy blond hair and blue eyes. Eyes that had been filled with dark intensity when he'd held her in his arms. Was it only a few weeks ago he'd kissed her?

Her lips tingled at the memory. Her body went warm all over as she recalled the sensation of being held in his arms, snuggled to his chest. Want, need, and desire melded together and curled through her. She'd never known a yearning so strong, so compelling, so consuming. So—

"If you don't flip those burgers soon, we can sell them to the National Hockey League for pucks."

Ashley dragged her gaze back to her mother. "Hmm?"

"Earth to Ashley." Her mother grinned. "I can't say I blame you. He's not hard on the eyes."

"Who?" She glanced at Max again. "Max? I was just trying to figure out why he's organizing the kids' games."

"Greg Karlik threw out his back."

Ashley laughed. "I'm going to hell for finding that amusing. Although it's not a surprise. The man doesn't bend. You can take the man out of the military. That doesn't mean you can take the military out of the man.''

''I know. But it seems Max had signed up to help with the kids because he was worried about gung-ho Greg and impressionable children. But now he's on his own.''

''How do you know all this?''

''Bernice,'' Jean said. ''She's his administrative assistant and pretty tight-lipped when it comes to business. But not the human interest stuff, thank goodness, or we couldn't be friends. And there are a lot of female humans who are interested in Max Caine.''

Including her. And she noted the smidgeon of jealousy jabbing through her at the mention of other females. Ashley glanced in his direction. He was bent at the waist talking to Cherry Addison's five-year-old blond moppet, Mary. The little girl removed his baseball hat, then put it on backwards and nodded her head in satisfaction. Max stood up straight and grinned down at the little girl, leaving his hat the way she'd put it. He blew his whistle and the kids took their places.

Ashley couldn't help smiling. ''And he seems to be doing a fine job on his own.''

''On many levels,'' Jean added.

Ashley's gaze snapped back to her mother. ''What does that mean?''

Jean calmly returned her look. She held up her hand and started ticking off things on her fingers. ''He's good with kids. He's a competent businessman. A good CEO. The changes he's made at CCC are small but positive. And if you're not already in love with him it's just a matter of time until you are.''

Her mother was right about all of the above. And it was annoying, because Ashley didn't want to be in love with any man, especially Max. "Then time is my friend because he'll be leaving soon."

"Has he said anything recently about that?"

"No. But when he first arrived he said he had a consulting contract right around Labor Day. The clock is ticking."

Jean's gaze narrowed on him. "In my department we're taking bets. My money's on him staying."

"Why?"

"I can't believe you haven't noticed the changes in him."

Unfortunately, Ashley had noticed. "You mean from the disastrous welcome reception where he looked as if he'd rather be having his legs waxed to organizing kids' games?"

"Yeah. The Pied Piper with an outstanding butt."

"Mother!"

"I'm old, not dead." Jean's grin was unapologetic. "The point is, if he doesn't leave, you're going to have to deal with your relationship hang-ups."

"Why? Even if he's around, it doesn't mean he's going to hang around me."

Jean snorted. "Have you ever heard the expression that if you bury your head in the sand, you leave your fanny exposed?"

"Yes, but—"

"At the very least Max is attracted to you. I happen to believe it's more than that."

"How can you be such a romantic?" Ashley demanded. "Love's been a big disappointment for you."

Jean adjusted her sun visor over her red curls, then

crossed one bare leg over the other. She was a very attractive woman, Ashley thought. Still trim in her denim shorts and sleeveless white cotton blouse.

"Just because romance hasn't worked out for me doesn't mean I don't believe in it. And my two brushes with disaster showed me what *not* to look for in a man. The way I look at it, those experiences weren't a complete waste. And I have you and Colleen to show for it."

"So you'd try again?" Ashley asked, surprised.

"You bet I would. As much as I love my girls, it's getting to be time for the two of you to be on your own. And I'd like to find someone for companionship and physical—"

Ashley held up her hand. "I can take it from there, Mom." She busied herself flipping burgers and turning hot dogs.

Jean laughed. "You're so easy, Ash. As much as I love watching you squirm, I'll leave it at that. But I don't see myself being alone. If someone interesting and hot comes along, I'd definitely give a relationship another try. And I like to think the third time's the charm."

"The charm for what?" Max asked.

He'd walked up to join them and reached into the tub of ice on the grass beside Ashley. After pulling out a canned soda, he popped the tab, then took a long drink.

He let out a long breath and looked at the two of them, waiting for an answer to his question.

"Nothing," Jean said. She stood up. "I have to go. Clint Johnson talked me into signing up for the volleyball tournament. I haven't played in years."

Her mother arched an eyebrow and Ashley got her message. She didn't know about interesting, but Clint Johnson was hot—for a mature man. Mentally, Ashley crossed her fingers that this would be her mother's charm.

"Have fun, Mom. Good luck." And she didn't mean on the volleyball court.

Max looked over the supplies on the picnic table. "Do we have enough of everything?"

"So far. But I'm expecting a run on food when the baseball game is over."

"Do you need help? I'm finished with the kids' activities."

She tipped her head. "Who are you and what have you done with Max Caine?"

"What?"

"When did you start playing well with others? What happened to the individualist with a chip on his shoulder? Now you're the poster child for interactive executives. I have to subtitle you—making it work in the workplace."

He propped a hip against the table beside her. "I don't know what you mean."

"I mean you've thrown yourself into this annual picnic."

"The employees deserve this day," he said simply. "They're what has made Caine Chocolate the solid business it is. Their loyalty has sustained growth for over eighty years. It's the least I can do."

"Sustainability isn't something I would expect you to find value in. You're the guy who hacks up corporations and sells off the pieces. What happened to the loner who kept to himself?"

"That's a good question."

"Let me know when you figure it out."

"You'll be the first," he said.

If he wasn't lying, he'd have to let her know pretty darn fast. Would her mother lose her bet? Would he go away for good?

"Max, are you staying?"

"Of course. After lunch is the water balloon toss. I need a partner by the way and I was hoping you'd do the honors."

"Sure." She sighed. "But that's not what I meant."

"Care to be more specific?"

When he smiled, her heart thumped painfully. Surely he could hear? With his hat backwards and a silly grin on his face, he looked carefree and so handsome she could hardly breathe. But she'd started this by asking the question. Not only did she have to take a breath, talking was now a necessity.

"Are you planning to take over for your grandfather and run the company?" When he looked at her without saying anything, she rushed to explain. "I'm curious because when you first got here, you said something about a consulting contract. Around Labor Day." She held out her hands. "Here we are."

He let out a long breath. "To be honest, I'm on retainer for that consulting job. I'm expecting the company's financial report any day now."

He lifted one broad shoulder in a casual shrug. After she managed to pull her gaze from the mouthwatering sight, she realized he'd told her absolutely nothing.

He stared at her for several moments. His gaze went from easygoing to intense as it settled on her mouth, sending her pulse rate through the roof. She wished they were somewhere more private. If wishes were…

Good grief, wishing had nothing to do with anything. She was a manager in his company. That should give her the right to a clue about his plans.

"What are you going to do?" she asked.

He sighed as he looked past her, to the cheers from the baseball field in the distance. Then he met her gaze and reached out to tuck a strand of hair behind her ear. "When I know, you'll know. You'll be the first."

"Promise?"

Good grief she sounded pathetic. She sounded as if it was personal. And the realization hit—it *was* personal. As hard as she'd tried to keep it from being that way, she cared what he was going to do. She cared in more than a businesslike way. She'd lost her objectivity. Although maybe she'd never had it in the first place.

He leaned down, kissed her lightly on the mouth, then whispered against her lips, "Promise."

The suddenly rough texture of his voice, the smile in his eyes when he looked at her, the tenderness in his touch when he traced her cheek with his finger—all added up to one thing. He was going to stay. Her heart did a happy little skip before she could stop it.

Her mother was right that Ashley was going to have to face her commitment issues head-on. She'd lived with an empty place inside her that she hadn't even realized was there until knowing Max, kissing him, wanting him. And maybe her mother was right about something else, too.

Maybe it *was* time to take a chance. Time to see if she could let down her guard.

* * *

When she heard a knock, Ashley looked up from the pile of paperwork in front of her. Her stomach dropped when she saw Max lounging in the doorway. His suit jacket was hanging by one finger and slung over his shoulder, giving him a rakish look that did funny things to her insides.

She smiled. ''Hi.''

''Hi, yourself.'' He walked in and rested a hip on the corner of her desk. Glancing at the watch on his wide wrist, he tsked loudly. ''It's past quitting time. Your employer should be ashamed of himself.''

''My employer is a serial workaholic and has no shame. He expects his worker bees to respect and emulate the example he sets.''

''Then I say we take him out back and beat the crap out of him.''

She set her pen down and leaned back in her chair. ''Okay. But tell whoever does the honors not to mess up his pretty face.''

''You think my face is pretty?'' he asked, arching an eyebrow.

''No. But your grandfather has a noble countenance that should be preserved.''

''I've been told I take after him.'' A fond smile turned up the corners of Max's mouth as he surveyed her workspace. ''So what are you working on?''

He dropped his jacket on the back of the chair in front of her desk, then walked to the corner of her office. He looked down at the display of prototype Valentine items. Chocolate cupids and arrows. Coffee mugs filled with foil-wrapped candy. Empty red foil heart boxes waiting to be filled.

Like her own heart before Max came back to town. It was certainly full these days. Happiness and hope were her two new best friends. Every day started with the anticipation of seeing Max. She couldn't stop that no matter how she tried.

"Looks good," he said, nodding at the items.

She stood and rounded her desk to move beside him. When her shoulder brushed his, a chorus line of tingles danced up and down her arm. "I especially like this chocolate greeting card."

"Nice," he said, tracing the cellophane-wrapped chocolate and the raised letters of the sentiment.

"I've got other messages in mind, some sweet, others a little racy. The usual like 'Be Mine' or 'I Love You' to 'Forever' and 'Later' or 'Tonight.'"

When his gaze met and held hers, Ashley saw something dark and exciting in his eyes. She felt a little flutter right beside her heart, something she felt only with him. She'd tried to ignore the sensation, but now she had to face it—because he would be around.

"So tell me, Ash. How can a woman who believes her love life is cursed put together such a romantic line of products?"

"It's called detachment. I'm very good at separating my professional and personal feelings."

"I'm not." His eyes darkened with hunger of the sensual kind. Intensity hardened the line of his jaw and pulled his mouth tight. He kicked her door closed with his foot, then slid his arm around her waist and drew her against him. "In fact, all day I've had something on my mind."

"Oh?"

"Oh, yeah," he said, lowering his lips to hers.

The joining of their mouths started a glow low in her belly. It spread outward across her flesh to tighten her breasts. He drew his tongue lightly across her bottom lip and she gave up and gave in to her hunger. She had no willpower where Max was concerned. She slid her hands over his chest to link her wrists behind his neck opening her mouth to admit him. The kiss deepened to a duel of lips and tongues. He tasted of passion and promise.

When he broke off the kiss, he sighed and touched his forehead to hers. ''Wow.''

''Well said.'' She drew in a shaky breath.

''Lady, you pack a powerful punch.''

''Is that good?''

''Very.'' He grinned. ''I'd like to stick around and let you punch me some more, but I've got to go.''

''Oh?''

''I'm having dinner with my grandfather.''

She was surprised at the depth of the disappointment that rumbled through her. Then he kissed the tip of her nose and let her go. When he stepped away from her, the absence of his touch made her feel cold.

''I see.''

''We have some things to discuss. Business,'' he said.

''Say hello to him for me.''

''I will.'' He picked up his jacket and slung it over his shoulder. ''Can I call you later?''

''Sure.''

''Good. Because I was going to anyway. Bye.'' He lifted a hand in parting, then he was gone.

Ashley sighed as she sat down behind her desk again. She'd wanted him to say straight out that he was her boss because he was permanently in charge. But probably that was one of the business items he needed to discuss with his grandfather. Even though he'd promised she'd be the first to know his plans, Max wouldn't say anything to anyone until it was official.

"Ashley, you worry too much," she said to herself.

The best thing she could do was bury herself in work to take her mind off things.

Much later, Bernice appeared in the doorway. "Ashley. Is Max around?"

"He left—" She glanced at the clock on the wall. "Wow, about two hours ago." She looked at Max's assistant. "What are you doing here so late?"

"Cleaning up my desk. I'm going on vacation next week."

That's right. Ashley would be covering for her. Then she noticed Bernice looked upset. "What's wrong?"

"I just took this message for him."

The pretty brunette frowned and handed her a piece of paper with notes scribbled on it. "One of our California-based competitors returned his call about a buyout. They're interested and want to speak with him."

Ashley felt as if she'd just taken a punch to the stomach. Blood roared in her ears. "Are you sure about that?" she managed to ask.

"Yes. It was an attorney for the company. He wasn't trying to be circumspect. He said Mr. Caine had contacted them regarding a merger, and they were interested in discussing the issue."

Ashley wondered if there was any color left in her

face. Stunned didn't begin to describe how she felt. How could she have been so wrong about Max? About all the signs?

"I'll make sure Mr. Caine gets the message, Bernice." She managed, just barely, to keep her voice even.

"Okay. Thanks, Ashley."

In a state of bewilderment, Ashley didn't know how long she sat there. She played the scenes over and over in her mind. Max making up with his grandfather. Bonding with the employees. Kissing her until her toes curled and she couldn't catch her breath. She'd only just let herself believe he wouldn't go, but the feeling of betrayal went soul deep. Because this whole time he'd been planning to sell the company out from under them. How dare he play with her feelings that way? And it wasn't just her. He'd played every employee in the company.

She stood suddenly. "You're not going to get away with this, Max."

Chapter Eleven

Three months ago if anyone had told Max he would be sitting in his grandfather's house drinking a brandy with the old guy, he'd have said they were crazy. But here he was. And even weirder—he was enjoying himself.

"So how are you feeling?" Max asked.

"Good." Bentley leaned over and set his snifter on the coffee table. When he straightened, he sighed. "Actually, I have a confession to make about my health."

"Let me guess. Your doctor cleared you to go back to work several weeks ago?"

Silver eyebrows rose. "Yes. How did you know?"

"Just a feeling."

"I can explain."

Max suppressed a grin. How many times had he said those same words in this room? He wouldn't be a teenager again for anything. But he had to admit, most of the time he'd deserved every consequence his grandfather had dished out. Finally, Max had the perspective to see that there had been just cause for the misunderstanding.

"I'm all ears," Max said.

Bentley cleared his throat. "The heart attack fortunately was a mild one. But when one is forced to face one's mortality, it gives one things to think about."

"I can imagine."

"Like what would happen to the company and all the people who depend on it for their livelihood." He held up a hand when Max started to speak. "You're my only family. I want you to take over for me. But based on our rocky past, I knew you'd say no. And I couldn't really blame you. To my astonishment, Ashley convinced you to stay until I recuperated or your work took you away." He sighed. "I recuperated too doggone fast. So I stretched the truth."

"You lied," Max said.

"Semantics." He waved a hand in dismissal, then stood and walked to the stone fireplace, resting a forearm on the mantel. "I hoped if you were here long enough you would learn to love Sweet Spring as I do. It was my wish that you would want the company that is your birthright."

"I don't know what to say," Max admitted.

"Thanks to Ashley I've already apologized for the past, but it doesn't seem like enough for what I did. We've never talked about it, Max."

"Maybe it's best not to."

"I don't agree. Maybe that heart attack was a blessing in disguise. For some reason I feel the need to get everything out in the open. So hear me out." He sighed. "I'm a stubborn man."

"Stubborn, opinionated, and dictatorial," Max murmured.

"Exactly."

He smiled. "I described you that way to Ashley the day I arrived. She told me the fruit doesn't fall far from the tree."

Bentley grinned. "She's right. I like that young woman."

"Me, too."

"The point is, being stubborn is an asset in the business world. The rest of the time, not so much." He walked over to the sofa and sat down again. "I told you I was sorry about what happened and I am. More than you can possibly know. But that's not all I regret. I was wrong to try to force your father into the family company when clearly he had chosen another course. I believed your father was misguided, making a mistake by turning away from his family responsibilities. It was a bone of contention between us. Then he died, and we never had a chance to clear the air."

"And I came to live with you."

He nodded. "Your grandmother raised your father practically single-handedly because I was busy running the company. It cost me time with her, with my family. Another of my many regrets. I loved her very much. After she died, I closed up and turned my energy into the business even more." He rested his elbows on his knees and clasped his fingers together. "I wasn't a very good father to my own son. Then you came to live with me after your parents died."

"Yeah."

The pain of loss wasn't sharp anymore. But Max would never forget the feelings of isolation and loneliness. He'd resented the fact that he'd had to stay with his grandfather. He'd wished he was old enough to live on his own and made a promise to become self-sufficient. He wouldn't need anyone.

"I loved your father. You won't know how much until you have a child of your own someday. I can't even describe the pain of losing him. And you lost your mother, too. I hadn't any idea how you felt. But there we were. An old man who didn't know the first thing about raising a boy, grieving the loss of his son while raising a kid who'd just suffered the devastating loss of both his parents. So I did what I do best." He met Max's gaze. "I buried myself in work."

"And I got into trouble. Probably to get your attention."

"It worked." Bentley grinned. "Especially that episode in the gym bathroom."

Max winced at the memory. Fortunately, no one had been hurt. But the place had been a mess. The consequences for that had put the brakes on his social life for a long time.

"Yeah." Max laughed. "Coach Harrington wanted me tarred and feathered for that one."

"The point is, whatever you set your mind to, you did well."

"So when there was industrial spying going on, you figured I was behind it."

He frowned. "Hindsight is twenty-twenty. If I'd been smarter, I'd have seen that all your shenanigans were nothing more than teenage indiscretions. When you worked at CCC you were always professional and smart as a whip. If I'd been less opinionated, I wouldn't have said the things I did."

"You're preaching to the choir, Grandfather. If I'd been less stubborn, I wouldn't have left without setting the record straight."

Ashley was right about that. If he'd stuck around, things could have been straightened out. Instead they'd wasted ten years.

Bentley shook his head. "Shouldn't have been necessary. You're a Caine. I should have known you wouldn't betray the company." He reached over and clapped a hand on Max's shoulder. "I don't want to make the same mistakes I made with your father. I'm sorry I ever doubted you. I love you, Max. And I'm grateful for this opportunity to tell you so. Thanks for sticking around. The fact is, it's good having you here. I figured if I told you the doctor cleared me to go back to work, you'd leave. So, I kept it to myself. I hope you're not angry."

Max cleared his throat against a sudden swell of emotion. "I'm not."

"Good."

"And since we're clearing the air, I think I owe you an apology for ignoring your olive branch all these years." Max sipped the last of his brandy. "Stubbornness is bad enough all by itself. But mix it with pride and the results are—"

"Pretty damn ugly," Bentley finished. "I'm tired and I don't have time to waste. I want to retire, Max. I want to stop and smell the roses. I'm giving you the company. Do with it what you will."

"But you'll stay on as an adviser," Max said. "Keep a hand in."

The older man shook his head. ''I don't want the responsibility. I meant what I said about selling it if you didn't stay. You'd be the best man for the job even if you weren't my grandson.''

''You don't know that—''

''I've followed your career. You're the man they call when a company is failing. Seems to me you can take what you've learned from that to keep it from happening at CCC.''

Max shook his head. ''You'd just walk away and turn it over to me?''

''I trust you, Max.'' His grandfather's faded blue eyes brimmed with sincerity. ''It's my greatest hope that you'll accept the offer. What do you say?''

Max didn't know what to say. He'd be stupid not to have known this was coming. But he hadn't expected the rush of personal feelings. This was so much more than just business. It was a family legacy. The blood, sweat and tears of Caines for upwards of eighty years were poured into the company. And his grandfather was entrusting it to him. Ten years ago he'd thought all his ties were severed beyond repair. But the truth was, his grandfather's validation was the piece always missing from his soul.

Max let out a long breath. ''I'd be lying if I said I hadn't thought about this. Ashley said—''

''Yes?'' Bentley arched one bushy silver brow inquisitively. ''Lovely girl. What did she say?''

''She's made me think about growing a company instead of taking it apart,'' he admitted.

She'd also made him think about twisted sheets and soft skin. Not to mention putting down roots and becoming a part of something enduring. No one knew better than Max that there was no such thing as permanent.

"Ashley is a smart girl. Good head for business. I've heard you've been spending a lot of time with her," Bentley said.

"From who?"

"I have my sources." His grandfather ran his fingers through his silver hair. "This is a small town. People are there for you if you need anything. But the price is that everyone knows your business—the good, bad and ugly. And they're going to talk about it."

"Believe it or not, I remember." Max had given them a lot to talk about.

"What I really want is for you to be happy. Can you do that in Sweet Spring?"

"I've been wondering the same thing."

More and more the thought of leaving opened up a mother lode of emptiness inside him. But that was all about Ashley. She gave meaning to his life. He was afraid he was in love with her.

His grandfather nodded knowingly. "Ashley's good for you."

"I agree."

"She reminds me of your grandmother. Same sweetness, but she's got a spine of steel. Maybe she can help you make up your mind to stay."

"There's still that consulting contract."

"So? Just do it. Then come back. CCC will be here waiting for you."

Was it really that easy? God, it sounded good. Being a part of something—the company as well as the town. And part of a couple. Coming home to Ashley every night. He'd thought she was all about her career—money and power. Boy was he wrong. She was one of a kind, with so many facets—career woman and consummate partner, in every conceivable way.

"What do you say, son?"

Max put his hand on his grandfather's shoulder. "I think it's the most attractive offer I've had in a very long time. I will give the matter my full attention and very serious consideration."

"Was that a yes?"

"Pretty damn close," Max admitted.

"Then on that note, I'm going to turn in."

Max looked at his watch. "It's only eight-thirty."

"My party days are over." He stood, his faded blue eyes twinkling. "But you're still in your prime. The night is young. You could call that young lady and do some spooning."

Max laughed. "Spooning?"

"You know, making out. Necking—"

"I get your drift, Grandad." He stood.

Bentley stared at him for a moment, then brushed his knuckle beneath his nose as he sniffled. "You haven't called me that in a very long time."

"Would you rather I didn't?"

"Not on your life." The older man shook his head and smiled, a suspicious brightness in his eyes.

Max swallowed hard, trying to dislodge the lump in his throat. Wait till Ashley heard about this. He had a lot to tell her. Somehow talking things over with her had become important to him. The need to see her as vital as air.

Ashley saw the lights in the guest house and knocked. She probably would have even if the place had been dark. She didn't think she'd ever been this angry, not even after finding out the guy she'd given up her scholarship for didn't care about her. She stoked the fire of her anger to keep the pain at bay. Max was an underhanded weasel and she intended to tell him so.

He answered the door and smiled when he saw her. The fact that her knees wobbled because of that smile increased her anger. As betrayed as she felt, how could he possibly affect her in such a visceral way?

"Come in. I was just thinking about calling you," he said, opening the door wide.

"Should my ears be burning?" Along with the rest of me, she thought, as she walked past him.

"As a matter of fact they should. Grandad—"

"Excuse me. You called him Grandad?"

Max rubbed the back of his neck as he shifted his feet. "Yeah. It just popped out. Another genuine Hallmark moment. I wish you'd seen it."

"Me, too," she said.

She should be happy about family bonding between the Caine men. If she hadn't just found out Max was a backstabbing Benedict Arnold, she would be. His grandfather would be pleased at the endearment, until he found out what his grandson was doing. She couldn't believe Mr. Caine knew and approved. If he did, his management team would have been apprised.

"So why were you talking about me?" she asked.

Some people counted to ten when they were so angry they wanted to rip someone's head off. She'd tried that on the drive over. No dice. She was struggling for control so she could be rational and reasonable when she ripped his head off.

"He said he knew you were responsible for convincing me to stick around."

That had been a mistake. In fact, she wished she'd refused to make the phone call that had brought him back. The leadership of the company might still be in question, but for her it would be business, not personal. Emotionally, she would be a lot better off.

Max grinned suddenly. "He's been playing possum."

"What do you mean?"

"He told me the doctor cleared him weeks ago to return to work."

Ashley shook her head. "Really?"

Again the fruit didn't fall far from the tree; they were both underhanded. But why wasn't she angrier with the senior Caine? Maybe because his subterfuge was all about trying to save the company—the wrong thing for the right reason. Wait until he found out putting his faith in Max had backfired. He would be devastated.

"He was buying time." Max slid his fingers into his pocket. "Funny thing. He always told me never to show weakness. Never admit you've made a mistake. But tonight he did both. He said he was wrong about my father and shouldn't have rushed to judgment about me."

Mr. Caine wasn't wrong this time, she thought. Max really was going to bring CCC down.

Max filled the silence. "I told him you think he and I are stubborn, opinionated and dictatorial."

That startled her. "What did he say?"

"That all those adjectives are absolutely accurate."

She was thinking other adjectives about him, too. Underhanded, deceitful, opportunistic.

"And he likes you," Max added.

"And your response?" Why should she care?

"I like you, too."

For just an instant, she thought he was sincere. Then she shook it off, refusing to be deceived again. He was continuing the charade. She'd wondered if he'd keep it up until he walked away. Now she had her answer and pain knifed through her.

"Did you two talk about anything else?" she asked.

"Yeah. As a matter of fact, I told him you've started me thinking about growing a company instead of taking it apart."

That might not be a total lie. He may have spent a minute or two thinking about it. Then discarded the idea.

He walked over to her and put his hands on her arms. His palms were warm and strong. For a second, before she could stop herself, she registered how good his touch felt. Then she shut down the feeling.

"Ash," he said, his gaze claiming hers, "he gave me the company. He entrusted it to me."

Max tried to pull her into his arms, but she pressed her palms against his chest, resisting him.

His brows drew together in a puzzled frown. "Ashley?"

"I really wish he hadn't done that."

"What are you talking about?"

"Everything you did said you were open to the idea of running the company. Growing it and expanding. People were reaching out to you, starting to trust you.

Accepting you. Because all of us believed you liked the idea of taking over for your grandfather."

"That's what I've been trying to tell you—"

"What you told me is that I'd be the first to know when you decided what you were going to do."

"Yeah. It's just one of the reasons I'm glad you came over. I've made a decision—" Max reached for her again, but she backed away.

"Just tonight you decided?"

"Yeah. I'm planning to—"

She held up a hand. "Tell me what's really going on, Max."

"What are you talking about?" The wary expression in his eyes turned hard, dark, intense.

"I have a message for you from the company in California you contacted about a possible buyout. You'll be happy to know they're interested."

"I don't know what you're talking about."

"No? You want me to believe you haven't been actively pursuing selling CCC?"

"That's the truth. I have no knowledge of anything like that."

"Then why would they say you had?"

"I can't answer that." His tone was curiously flat, devoid of emotion.

"Can't? Or won't?" This denial was nothing more or less than what she'd expected. Righteous anger expanded inside her. "I believed you when you said you'd give me a heads up about the future of the company. You strung me along. You made me care—"

Darn it. She thought she had it together enough to

confront him. Obviously she'd been wrong or that wouldn't have slipped out.

They stared at each other for several moments. She wasn't sure what she expected until he said nothing. Why didn't he tell her she was wrong? That there was some mistake? Why did his eyes look so empty?

Ashley huffed out a breath. "Don't you have anything to say for yourself?"

"Why bother?" A muscle in his jaw contracted. "You've already made up your mind. Déjà vu all over again. You've assumed the worst. Some things never change. I guess you really can't go home again."

"Max, tell me that—"

He walked over to the door and opened it. "There's nothing left to say."

He was probably right. She moved to the doorway and glanced up at his face. Without the haze of her fury, she saw him clearly. The emptiness in his expression made her shiver.

She stood on the porch. "Max—"

"Goodbye, Ashley." He shut the door—quietly.

Now that her legendary redheaded temper was spent and her adrenaline rush was gone, she had nowhere to hide. No way to camouflage her feelings. The coldness in his voice froze her heart. The lack of emotion when he'd dismissed her said loud and clear it was goodbye forever. The pain of that realization sliced all the way to her soul.

Ashley trailed behind Chip into the living room after being summoned to the estate by Mr. Caine. Following a sleepless night, she'd been grateful it was Saturday, giving her the weekend to prepare herself for whatever was going on at the office. Then she'd received the call and she'd broken speed limit laws in her haste to get here.

"Chip, is there something wrong with Mr. Caine? Is he ill?"

"I don't know, Miss Gallagher. He's upset. I don't believe I've ever seen him so agitated. He ordered me to phone you and ask you to come over. That's all I know."

They walked into the living room. "Miss Gallagher to see you, sir."

"Thank you, Chip. Please leave us alone."

"As you wish, sir." The butler pulled the doors closed when he left.

Bentley Caine had always looked far younger than his age. But today, standing by the fireplace, every one of his seventy plus years showed in the lines on his face and in the stooped, defeated slump of his shoulders. Max must have talked to him, confessed what he was up to. He knew Ashley would talk to his grandfather about it.

"Ashley, what did you say to Max?"

"Me?"

He nodded. "He's packing to catch a flight to L.A. When I asked him why, he said you would know."

Even after what Max had done, her heart caught at the news that he was leaving. And of course Mr. Caine would be upset. But apparently Max wanted her to break the bad news.

"Sir, you might want to sit down."

He shook his head. "What happened?"

"I got a message at work indicating Max was putting out the word that Caine Chocolate could be bought. I confronted him about it.'' She shrugged. ''I suppose he figured since the cat was out of the bag, it was time for him to go.''

''Oh, no.'' Then the older man walked over to the sofa and slowly lowered himself to the cushy softness.

She didn't like the ashen cast to his face. ''What is it, Mr. C.?''

''It wasn't Max. I put out feelers about a potential sale.''

''Oh, no.'' On legs that would barely hold her weight, Ashley moved to sit beside him.

''It was right after Max returned, before I was sure I could trust him with the company, before I knew there was a chance he would stay. I thought it was best to cover all my options. Since I had time on my hands, I made some phone calls. Max didn't know anything about it.''

''Why didn't you say something to the management staff?''

''Any information was supposed to be channeled through legal—or me. There was no reason to start a company panic. Hell, a town panic.''

''If only I'd known—'' She closed her eyes for a moment as the enormity of what she'd done swept over her.

''Last night Max and I had a good talk,'' he said. ''He all but said he would accept my offer.''

She remembered now that Bernice had said the message was for Max. She'd jumped to conclusions then planted the seed in Ashley's mind. Anger and hurt had kept Ashley from thinking it through.

''I'm so sorry. I didn't know. The message said they were returning Mr. Caine's call. I thought it was Max.

I know how you feel about the company. It never occurred to me you would sell. I automatically assumed—''

''You know what they say when you assume?''

''Yes.'' It makes an ass out of *u* and *me.* ''In our conversations, Max told me selling out would be best. I just thought—'' Even though everything he'd done had shown her something different.

''It's just like ten years ago. My only consolation is that this time I wasn't the one who misjudged him.'' Blue eyes full of sadness met her own gaze. ''I thought I had my family back. It would have been nice.''

His resignation and sadness started a trembling that spread through her. Defeat wasn't like him and it worried her. She would have felt better if he'd been angry with her.

''I'll talk to him, sir. It won't be like the last time.''

''I'm afraid the damage has been done, Ashley.'' He stood and left the room.

He was wrong. She would talk to Max, apologize for being an idiot. For Mr. C.'s sake, she had to convince him not to go. The fact that she was in love with Max didn't matter. She didn't have a snowball's chance in hell of making him believe that.

Her heart was already broken; that was her own fault. She would learn to live with it. But she couldn't live with herself if she didn't do something to keep Max from breaking his grandfather's heart.

Chapter Twelve

Max closed his suitcase and wished he could tuck his feelings away as easily as he had his boxers and socks. The last time he'd left, he'd been certain the red clay dirt of Sweet Spring, Texas, would never touch his shoes again. If only he'd been right. His anger was stronger than before, although anger was too passive a word to describe the acid burning through him. Apparently, he couldn't go home again. Stupid to think he could live down his reputation. But Ashley had made him believe it could be different.

He picked up his two bags and set them by the front door. Just as he turned away, a knock sounded. He was tempted to ignore it, but thought his grandfather might want one more shot at convincing him not to go. His gut clenched at the thought of leaving, because after all these years, the two of them had finally connected.

But when Max glanced through the window, Ashley

was standing there. Anger and hurt, pain and need roared through him. He was pretty sure his grandfather was behind this visit; the old man didn't know she was the last person who could convince him to stay. But Max figured he owed it to Bentley to at least listen to her. Besides, this was different from last time. He wasn't running away. He would see the old man. Just because he couldn't stay and take over the company didn't mean he would break the bond they'd repaired.

He opened the door and leaned his shoulder against the doorframe—a casual pose that was a lie. He felt more like a spring wound too tightly. "Ashley. You're the last person I expected to see."

"Your grandfather called me. He said you're leaving town."

"Did you tell him why?"

"Yes."

"I'd invite you in, but—" Even now he still wanted her. How stupid was that? He looked at the watch on his wrist. "I have to catch a plane to L.A."

She twisted her fingers together. "I'd appreciate it if you'd listen to what I have to say."

"Do as I say, not as I do?"

His only excuse for stooping to childish character assassination was that he was too angry to be rational. She'd misjudged him the same way his grandfather had, but this was so much worse. And it shouldn't be. Ten years ago he'd had nothing when he walked away. Now he had a life in place. But it was worse because Ashley had shown him what a life with color and companionship and caring was all about.

"You're implying I wouldn't listen, but you didn't even attempt to tell me I was wrong," Ashley said.

''There was no point. You had me tried and convicted.''

''I drew a logical conclusion because you made no secret of the fact that you believed selling the company was the best thing to do.''

He'd changed his mind about that. For all the good it did. ''I also told you I would tell you when I decided what to do. But you didn't trust me.''

''I—'' She took a small step forward. ''Max, I was an idiot. I jumped to the wrong conclusion.''

''Yeah, you did. So is that it?''

She blinked. ''No that's not it. We're not finished yet.''

''Aren't we?'' He arched one eyebrow. ''What's left to say?''

''A lot. I want to explain why I was an idiot.''

He ran his fingers through his hair. ''Don't tell me. Curse of the Gallagher women.''

''Partly,'' she agreed.

''You gave me a lot of grief for leaving town ten years ago without talking things over. Yet you tried and convicted me without letting me put up a defense. No benefit of the doubt for past offenders. You jumped to conclusions.''

''It felt like you lied to me. And my temper kicked in. When that happens, there's not a whole lot of room left for common sense.''

''I see.''

''I don't think you do.'' She held her hands out in a helpless gesture. ''I've been so focused on not making another relationship mistake, subconsciously I was looking for something in your negative column.''

"You didn't have to look so hard. I've got numerous flaws to choose from."

"I know."

One corner of his mouth quirked up. "Don't sugarcoat it, Ash. Tell me how you really feel."

"I'm trying," she said, her tone laced with frustration. "The truth is I'm falling in love with you…."

She stopped and glanced away for a moment. The pink creeping into her cheeks told him she hadn't meant to reveal that. He wanted to ask her to repeat it, but figured it was irrelevant to this discussion. And his life.

"Max, the truth is these feelings scare me. So when I got the message at the office, I went from zero to furious and grabbed on with both hands. It was something I could use to push you away. I was so prepared for something bad, I never questioned it."

"I'm glad I didn't disappoint you," he said.

"It's not you, it's me. I had to believe men leave, Max. That it's in their nature. Otherwise it means that I'm not enough to make them stay. Your grandfather told me he's the one who made inquiries about a possible buyout. I'm very sorry I misjudged you."

He slid his hands into the pockets of his slacks because, the truth was, he wanted to pull her into his arms. And that didn't make any sense.

Her gaze darted over his face, waiting for his response. But he didn't have anything to tell her.

Finally, she said, "When rational thought returned, I realized all the vibes you were giving off indicated you were planning to take over running the company." She glanced at the suitcases by the door and the look in her eyes went from pleading to desperate.

"Don't go, Max. You like it here. I could see that. You found something that was missing in your life. I think that's why you came back in the first place."

"It doesn't matter why I came back."

"Yes, it does. Don't cut off your nose to spite your face."

"Look, Ashley. There's nothing you can say that will change my mind."

"What about this—I'm going to the office to turn in my resignation."

"What?"

"I'm quitting."

That got his attention. "But—you worked hard to earn that position. What about money and power?"

"Some things are more important. Like family." She sighed. "I'll get another job. But you need to take over the company for your grandfather. You can do that if I'm not there. If you leave again, it will break his heart. I'm responsible for this mess. I'll go."

"Is that all you have to say?"

"No. There's one more thing. It takes one to know one."

Was that payback for his "do as I say, not as I do" remark? "What's that supposed to mean?"

"You're running away again."

"No, I—"

"You're afraid to care because every time you do, it costs you. Makes it hard to commit when you're waiting for the other shoe to drop. You know it will hurt." She took a deep breath. "But it's time to stop running, Max. If not for yourself, then for your grandfather. And all the people in this town who depend on the Caines and the company."

Max didn't respond, so he saw the precise moment when the flame of hope in her eyes sputtered and died.

"That's all I have to say." She let out a long breath. "Probably it was too much. One of my many flaws. Have a good flight, Max." She turned away and walked down the steps.

Max shut the door, then hit the wall with his fist. Why the hell did she do that? And he didn't mean coming here to talk. Why did she get to him, make him feel like a bastard? She went straight for the gut; she knew right where to aim. He'd never expected involvement with her to be more than superficial. And he wasn't sure when it had deepened. Maybe the first day he'd been back. When they'd looked for his Grandad and she'd advised him not to describe the restaurants as hotbeds of heart disease. Or it could have been her need to quickly leave his office when he'd told her she was the reason he stayed. It might have been her passionate defense of everything and everyone important to her.

Was he important to her? Did she mean what she'd said about loving him? He shook his head. What did it matter now? He was leaving. Somehow he had to find a way to forget about Ashley Gallagher.

He was afraid that would be like trying not to breathe.

Ashley stopped outside the CCC conference room. Mr. Caine was meeting with the representatives of a company interested in buying him out. She'd turned in her resignation, telling him Max might come back if she were gone. But he'd refused it. He'd told her he would find another way to bring his grandson home. That was a month ago and Max still wasn't home.

She stood there for several moments, staring at the heavy wooden door. She'd wished for money and power on her birthday. Her promotion was supposed to be her opportunity, her wish come true. Losing Max had made her realize money and power weren't what she really wanted. Why did lessons have to hurt this much? No Caine, no gain. No happiness.

Suddenly the door opened and several men, all in business suits, walked out, followed by Bentley Caine. He shook hands with all of them and said, "I'll be in touch."

"We'll be waiting." The tall, distinguished-looking man with brown hair, silver at the temples, seemed to be their spokesman.

Mr. Caine watched the contingent leave, then met her gaze. "Ashley."

"Bernice said you wanted to see me."

He nodded. "Go in the conference room."

"Is the meeting over, sir?"

"That one is," he said, staring at the delegation waiting for the elevator at the end of the hall.

"What happened?"

"You mean am I selling out?"

"Yes."

He shrugged and angled his head toward the door. "Go on in now."

"Is there another meeting?"

He nodded, but his eyes twinkled. "A most important one."

So this is what the beginning of the end felt like, she thought. She couldn't feel much of anything. For her, the end had come the day Max left. Maybe she was numb from dealing with that, because it was hard to work up emotion about losing the company. She couldn't imagine anything worse than losing Max. She felt the pain and emptiness of it clear to the depths of her soul. After that, this was just a job. She'd find another one. Although she couldn't help feeling guilty about all the other employees who would be forced to look for work.

She opened the door and went inside. The room held a large, rectangular conference table surrounded by wooden chairs with seats and backs covered in a blue-gray tweed. Fluorescent lights hummed overhead. At the far end was a sofa table holding a vase of carnations, star lilies, roses and baby's breath. Beside that stood a man, his back to her.

Her knees went weak when she realized she knew that back. "Max—"

He turned. "Hi."

"What are you doing here?" she asked, her heart pounding, her knees going weak.

There was nothing wrong with his knees she thought, as he strode toward her. He stopped an arm's length away and stared down at her. "My grandfather was involved in negotiations and asked me to be here."

"I'm sure he was pleased you came."

"He was."

So was she. And she wanted to ask him what had happened in the talks, but the blood was pounding in her ears. All she could do was stare, drink in the sight of him. The sandy hair, blue eyes, chiseled features, square jaw—it was a strong face, the face of a good man. A face she'd missed terribly.

"The company's going to be okay," he said. "No one is going to lose their job. Grandad has figured out a way to keep it. He's not going to sell."

"That's really good news."

He reached out and gently nudged her chin up with his knuckle, forcing her to meet his gaze. "There's something else I have to tell you. I hope you'll think it's good news, too."

"What?"

"I've missed you, Ash. I've had a lot of time to think about what you said, and you were right. I *was* running. It doesn't take a shrink to see that my whole life is about being on the move. It's hard to hit a moving target. The thing is, I knew this. I just never found anyone who made me want to stay in one place. But you—" He shook his head and rubbed his palm across the back of his neck. "You scared the hell out of me."

"Should I be flattered or insulted?"

"Definitely flattered. I've avoided putting down roots for fear of getting hammered again. But it happened anyway."

"Roots? Or the getting hammered part?"

"Both. I guess I needed to leave to understand what I had. Until you, I was content alone. Now I can't be content without you." One corner of his mouth quirked up.

"Oh, Max—" Her voice caught. "After what I did to you?"

"No one knows better than me that people make mistakes. If I've learned anything from the past, it's to face things head-on. A very wise woman once told me it takes a special kind of rude to refuse an apology. I refused yours. But I've come back to accept it. I love you, Ash."

She couldn't believe it. "I didn't dare hope to hear you say that."

"So it's good news?"

"The best. And I love you, too. I know your job takes you all over, but I'll follow you anywhere."

"You'd do that?" he asked, his gaze searching hers. "Even though it would mean leaving your family? And all your ties in the community?"

She nodded. "When you left, I found out all the roots in the world won't make me happy without you." She stared up at him. "You make me happy."

He cupped her face in his hands, then lowered his head and touched his lips to hers in a tender kiss full of promises. When he pulled back, he said, "You are an amazing woman."

"Does that mean you'll take me with you?"

"That won't be necessary."

She frowned. "Why not?"

"I'm the solution Grandad found for the company. He gave it to me, and I'm going to run it."

"But the meeting—"

"It wasn't about selling." He smiled.

Then she didn't care what it was about. Everything was going to be all right because Max was back to stay. "You're going to be my boss permanently? And I was so afraid I'd never see you again."

"I've been looking for you all my life. It wouldn't be especially bright to turn my back now."

"But we knew each other ten years ago," she protested.

"You were too mature for me, then. I had to grow up. Believe it or not, you helped me with that. So actually this is all your fault," he teased. "If it doesn't go well, you're to blame. You're the one who made me want to stay put."

"I didn't know I had such power." She thought about the night of her birthday and smiled. "I think my wish just came true, but it has nothing to do with money and power."

"Don't be so sure," he said. "If you marry me, what's mine is yours. You'll have more money than you know what to do with."

"And power?"

He put his arms around her and snuggled her against him. "You have the power to make me the happiest man in Sweet Spring, Texas, if you'll say yes and marry me."

"With all my heart, yes." She smiled.

"You know, you're not especially good at flirting." He grinned. "But your kisses are sweeter and have more oomph than a triple fudge truffle."

She would show him who couldn't flirt. Standing on tiptoe, she tilted her mouth up for his kiss. "So what are you waiting for?"

"Not a darn thing."

He touched his lips to hers and she flirted with the boss to her heart's content.

* * * * *

Don't miss Jordan's story in
the final installment of
Teresa Southwick's miniseries,
IF WISHES WERE...
Three friends, three birthdays,
three loves of a lifetime!
AN HEIRESS ON HIS DOORSTEP
Silhouette Romance #1712
Available March 2004

Discover what happens
when wishes come true
in

A brand-new miniseries
from reader favorite

Teresa Southwick

Three friends, three birthdays,
three loves of a lifetime!

BABY, OH BABY!
(Silhouette Romance #1704, Available January 2004)

FLIRTING WITH THE BOSS
(Silhouette Romance #1708, Available February 2004)

AN HEIRESS ON HIS DOORSTEP
(Silhouette Romance #1712, Available March 2004)

Available at your favorite retail outlet.

Visit Silhouette at www.eHarlequin.com SRIWW

COMING NEXT MONTH

#1710 MAJOR DADDY—Cara Colter

When five adorable, rambunctious children arrived on reclusive Cole Standen's doorstep, his much needed R and R was thrown into upheaval. But just when things were back to the way he liked them (ie. under his control!), Brooke Callan, assistant to the children's famous mother, arrived. Could Brooke and the brood of miniature matchmakers rescue this hero's wounded heart?

#1711 DYLAN'S LAST DARE—Patricia Thayer

The Texas Brotherhood

Pregnant physical therapist Brenna Farren was not going to let her newest patient, handsome injured bull rider Dylan Gentry, give up on his recovery *or* talk her into entering a marriage of convenience with him! But soon she found herself in front of a judge exchanging I dos—and getting a whole different kind of "physical therapy" from her heartthrob husband!

#1712 AN HEIRESS ON HIS DOORSTEP—Teresa Southwick

If Wishes Were…

Jordan Bishop fantasized about being a princess and living in a palace. But when her secret birthday wish was answered with…*a kidnapping,* she was rescued by the sexiest innocent bystander she'd ever seen. She found herself in his castle—and in the middle of a *big* misunderstanding! Could the love-wary Texas oil baron who saved the day be Jordan's prince?

#1713 THE SECRET PRINCESS—Elizabeth Harbison

The princess was alive! And she was none other than small-town bookstore owner Amy Scott. Despite her protests, Crown Prince Wilhelm insisted the skeptical American beauty return to Lufthania with him. But while Amy was sampling the royal lifestyle, Wil found himself wanting to sample Amy's sweet kisses….

SRCNM0204